From a young age, Nyrae Dawn dreamed of growing up and writing stories. For years she put her dream on hold. Nyrae worked in a hospital emergency room, fell in love and married one of her best friends from high school. In 2004 Nyrae, her husband and their new baby girl made a move from Oregon to Southern California and that's when everything changed. As a stay-at-home mom for the first time, her passion for writing flared to life again. She hasn't stopped writing since. With two incredible daughters, an awesome husband and her days spent writing what she loves, Nyrae considers herself the luckiest girl in the world. She still resides in sunny Southern California, where she loves spending time with her family and sneaking away to the bookstore with her laptop. Nyrae Dawn also writes adult romance under the name Kelley Vitollo.

To find out more about Nyrae Dawn, visit www.nyraedawn.com. Find her on Facebook at nyraedawnwrites and follow her on Twitter @NyraeDawn.

ALSO BY NYRAE DAWN AND
PUBLISHED BY HEADLINE ETERNAL

What a Boy Wants
What a Boy Needs

THE GAMES TRILOGY
Charade
Façade

Nyrae Dawn

WHAT A BOY WANTS

headline
ETERNAL

Copyright © 2012 Nyrae Dawn

The right of Nyrae Dawn to be identified as the
Author of the Work has been asserted by her in accordance
with the Copyright, Designs and Patents Act 1988.

First published in Great Britain in 2013 by HEADLINE ETERNAL
An imprint of HEADLINE PUBLISHING GROUP

1

Apart from any use permitted under UK copyright law,
this publication may only be reproduced, stored, or transmitted,
in any form, or by any means, with prior permission in writing of the
publishers or, in the case of reprographic production, in accordance
with the terms of licences issued by the Copyright Licensing Agency.

All characters in this publication are fictitious and any resemblance
to real persons, living or dead, is purely coincidental.

Cataloguing in Publication Data is available from the British Library

ISBN 978 1 4722 0874 3

Typeset in Electra by Palimpsest Book Production Limited,
Falkirk, Stirlingshire

Printed and bound in Great Britain by
CPI Group (UK) Ltd, Croydon, CR0 4YY

Headline's policy is to use papers that are natural, renewable
and recyclable products and made from wood grown in sustainable
forests. The logging and manufacturing processes are expected to
conform to the environmental regulations of the country of origin.

HEADLINE PUBLISHING GROUP
An Hachette UK Company
338 Euston Road
London NW1 3BH

www.eternalromancebooks.co.uk
www.headline.co.uk
www.hachette.co.uk

To my husband. I can write romance because you taught me what love is.

CHAPTER ONE

There was nothing better than opening my email to a job offer. Well, I could think of a few things I liked more, but money wise, this topped the list. Another love-struck girl, in desperate need of my services. And another hundred bucks in my pocket. Sweet!

To: Hook-up Doctor <hookup_doctor@yahoo.com>
From: PA Rocks <icantbelieveididthis@yahoo.com>
Subject: Boy help?
Dear Mr. Hook-up Doctor,

I snorted. Mr. Hook-up Doctor? That was a first. I'd been at this for six months now, and I had yet to be called Mr. anything.

I kind of liked it.

Maybe I'd start using it from now on. It made my business sound more legit. Like I was one of those guys in a suit, sitting in a high-rise office in some big city, instead of a broke, seventeen-year-old with no wheels. I could definitely get used to that fantasy.

Except . . . I'm not really a suit kind of guy. It would be my high-rise office, though. I could wear whatever the hell I wanted. I was thinking jeans and t-shirts as the required uniform. Oh, and Vans. Have to have the Vans.

I twisted the ring in my eyebrow and looked down at my laptop again. I could figure that crap out later. My fundage was running low, and an email to my Hook-up Doctor account meant possible money. Money meant a car. Cars equaled more chicks. You get the picture.

> *Mr. Hook-up Doctor,*
> *Umm, yeah. This is weirder than I thought it would be. I'm sure you get that a lot. I'm really not like the other girls who need your help, though. Well, not that I know any girls who have come to you, but I'm not the kind of girl who usually does something like this. Ugh! I'm rambling, aren't I?*

"No, shit. What was your first clue?" I groaned.

Okay, sorry. I'm just not used to emailing someone to get a guy. I'm the sensible one. I don't need someone to help me with boys. Not that I'm a compulsive dater or anything, and well, I guess it's obvious I need help since I'm emailing you, but this is different. What I'm trying to say is, I'm not the kind of girl who would usually give a guy who wasn't into her the time of day. Damn, I'm rambling again. Sorry.

I don't really know what kind of information you need, so yeah, I'll end this painful email. I just wanted to see if you're available to help. This guy, well, he's kind of out of my league. Not like he thinks he's too good for me, it's just . . . yeah, he's not the kind of guy who dates a girl like me. Can you help? What's the next step? Your blog isn't really too forthcoming on information, you know.

Hope to hear from you soon!

PA Rocks (This whole process is confidential, right?)

Shaking my head, I leaned back in my computer chair and kicked my feet up on the desk. Pulling a dart out of the arm of my chair, I tossed it at the dartboard on my wall.

See? This was a classic example of why girls don't get the guys they want. We don't like that wishy-washy, back and forth crap. Girls need to decide who they are: either the strong, confident chick who puts us on our ass and still makes us want more, or the shy girl next door who we want to either corrupt or bring home to our parents. A toss-up.

Or, there were those girls in between. When I say in between, I don't mean they're all over the place like PA, but they're not the man-eater girls or the completely innocent ones, either. They know who they are. They're confident in a more quiet way. They're subtle, not pushy like Black Widow Girl or too standoffish like Little Miss Innocent, they're . . . cool.

Unfortunately, you don't run into the latter girl too often. And honestly, when guys do, a lot of the time we don't notice her. Sucks, but true.

I threw another dart at the board. My finger lingered over the mouse. Without letting myself think too much about it, I hit reply.

> *Miss PA,*
> *I usually don't do this, but I'm going to give you a small piece of free advice. Then, we*

can talk details and see if you want to go through with this. I can tell you right now why you don't have the guy you want. Make up your mind about who you are. Half the email you were all, I-am-woman-hear-me-roar. And the rest of the time, you were the unsure chick who stumbles over her words and hides in the corner of the gym during the dances. We're guys. Half the time, we don't know who we are. It helps things become a lot easier if we know who you are.

I can hear you now, and before you go all She-Woman on me, let me tell you, I know it's a double standard. I will fully admit crap like that goes on. You know, the whole "life's not fair" thing. Nothing we can do about it. I didn't make the rules, I just know them.

That advice was free. I usually don't do that (a guy has to make money). From now on, everything costs.

Anyway, yes, this is confidential. I don't want anyone knowing who I am any more than you do (hence the whole 007 email thing).

My services are a hundred bucks. I know that seems like a lot, but you're trying to score your dream guy here. I'm worth it.

I promise. I take fifty dollars up front and fifty after. You don't pay the last fifty if you don't get the guy (it's never happened). I'll give you instructions later on how to pay. What I need you to do is decide if you want to continue. If so, I really need you to think about which of those girls you are and let me know. Each of my clients get a personalized plan of action, so I need to know about who you are and a little about the guy. No names. Make up some kind of code name for him (please, no hottie, cutie etc. A guy can only take so much). I don't need to know his date of birth, hair color and favorite thing to do on a first date or anything. I'm talking basics here.

Hope to hear from you soon.
Hook-up Doctor

Pushing out of my chair, I pulled my t-shirt over my head and tossed it into the pile of clothes next to my guitar. One clean shirt later, I was out the door, jogging down the stairs, and hoping to make it out of the house before—

"Sebastian Dale Hawkins! Where are you going? I told you Roger was coming over tonight. He really wants to meet you." *Shit*. The full name and everything.

My mom walked around the side of the stairs, crossed her arms and glared at me, still wearing her "Courtney's Dance Studio" shirt. Yes, my mom taught dance, but not the sleazy kind. If I had a dollar for every time someone made a wise crack about it, I wouldn't need to be The Hook-up Doctor at all.

"Ma, why does he want to meet me? I mean, it's not like I'm five years old and looking for a daddy." I might sound harsh, but it was always the same thing. She met a new guy and we had to play house. After seventeen years, I was pretty sick of it.

"Because he's a nice guy? Because we're in a serious relationship, and you're my son? Come on, Sebastian. I really think he might be the one." My mom's bottom lip poked out like she was a toddler trying to get her way. Or, hell, maybe that was just a girl thing. I'd file that bit of information away for later. Might be something I could use as The Hook-up Doctor.

I had to say, she knew what she was doing. My mom was good. For teaching people how to get what they want, I obviously learned from the best. But after a while, I also learned how to say no to her. "I can't. You know I would, but I have this project I have to work on with Aspen. I'm heading over there right now."

"Why are you going there? I know she'd rather be over here than snacking on tofu burgers at her house."

It's hard to bullshit a bull-shitter. By the way Mom narrowed her brown eyes at me, I knew she wasn't buying what I was trying to sell her. "I'm going over there, and then she's driving me to meet up with Jaden and Pris. It's a group . . . project . . . thing." She gave me those all-knowing eyes that made it hard to lie to her.

"Next time?" she pleaded.

"Sure." I let the lie roll off my tongue. I had no desire to meet this guy. What was the point? The four husbands before him weren't the one, and I doubted he was either. Still, I pulled her into a hug, because I knew she'd just let me off the hook on purpose and yeah, I'm a guy and I love my mom. So shoot me. I'm man enough to hug her without feeling like a mama's boy.

After a quick squeeze, she finally let me go. "Oh, and, Sebastian? It's Friday night before the last week of school. Going out with your friends would have been a more believable excuse than a group project thing." My mom winked at me.

I'm an idiot.

I pulled on my Vans and slipped out. It took me about thirty seconds to walk two doors down to

Aspen's. Her house was the only one on the block painted a different color. Her front door was orange. Who would do that?

I raised my hand to knock, but her mom pulled it open before my fist came in contact with the door. And here was the very person who would have an orange front door.

"Come in, Sebastian. Phil's meditating," she whispered, and I fought some serious eye-rollage. "Sneak upstairs. Aspen is in her room—unless, you need to be centered? I'm sure Phil wouldn't mind if you joined him." She smiled all hopeful-like and I really hated to deflate her excitement, but not as much as I disliked the idea of being centered.

With a shake of my head, I tip-toed up the stairs, realizing I should have gone to her window. Her room faced the backyard, and their gate was always unlocked. Aspen has begged me a million times to hike the side of the mountain that was her house, instead of using the front door. I think her parents embarrassed her, and I could see why, but it always felt too *Dawson's Creek* for me. The fact that I knew a show that had been off the air for years well enough to know climbing through her window was too Dawson/Pacey-like, made the whole window thing an even bigger hell no. I blamed it on that Katie chick marrying

Tom Cruise. I might have to start rethinking the Spiderman thing if it came down to finding my inner feng shui or climbing a damn trellis.

Aspen's door was half open, so instead of knocking, I slipped it open slowly, pulled some more twinkle-toe walking like I'd done on the stairs and grabbed her shoulders. "Boo!"

"Ahh!" She jumped, slammed her laptop closed and whirled around, her honey-brown ponytail flying out and almost poking me in the eye. She gave me that pissed-off Aspen look, and I knew I was screwed. "What the hell, Sebastian! You scared the crap out of me."

Yeah, I knew I was a punk, but I couldn't help it. I laughed. "That was classic. You looked like you were going to pee your pants." She punched me in the arm, and I laughed louder.

"Shut up." She leaned backward against her desk, with a hand on her laptop.

"Don't pout, Woodstock. You can't help that I'm stealthy as a ninja."

She pushed past me, bright green eyes throwing daggers my way as she picked her cell phone up off the bedside table. I ignored her dirty looks and flopped down on her bed, kicking my feet up on the purple comforter. "We should probably wait a few minutes before we bail. Daddy Peace is meditating, and your mom already tried to get me to do it, too. I'm sure she wouldn't let you escape quite as easily as she did me."

"See! That's why I tell you to come in the window. All you had to do is climb that lazy butt of yours up the side of the house, let me know you were here, and then I could have snuck out. Now she'll be watching for me." Aspen sat down at the foot of her bed. She was a t-shirt and jeans kind of girl, but when she leaned over to tie her shoes, I caught a glimpse of smooth, creamy skin right above her jeans that had me wondering for the first time what she'd look like if she decided to show a little more flesh every now and again.

I didn't *like* her because—well, I didn't really do the whole "like" thing. I did the fun thing, and I didn't think Aspen would be down for that. There were way too many chicks in the proverbial sea to ruin a friendship for a sliver of skin, anyway. "Oh, I see. So I have to scale your house, and you get to sneak out the front door?"

"Now you're getting it. See how smart you are?" she teased back.

"Aw, you think I'm smart? That's so nice of you to say." I crossed my arms, waiting for her next comeback.

"No, I think you're cocky."

"Yeah, that's what Stephanie said, too—ouch!" I covered the family jewels as she attacked me with her other shoe. "Settle down, woman. You're violent!" I chuckled as her dainty little shoe hit me in the thigh.

"Men," she mumbled. "I've had about enough of conceited guys today."

She stopped hitting me, and I sat up next to her, nudging her with my shoulder. "What's wrong, Woodstock?"

She used to hate it when I called her that, but over the years, she'd gotten used to it. I couldn't help it. Her parents were tree-hugging hippies. Not that I had anything against that, but they were always telling us stories about their peace and love adventures. They're not old enough to have gone to Woodstock or anything, but it made for easy jokes.

"Nothing."

She tried to stand up, but I pulled her back down by the wrist. I gave her crap, but if any other guy did it, I'd kick his ass. If he was bigger than me, Jaden would help, too. That was what our group did. We always backed each other up. "Seriously. Did something happen?"

Her cell phone beep cut off our conversation.

Aspen flipped it over. "It's Jaden." Half her mouth kicked up in a smile. Obviously, she was just as excited about going out tonight as I was. "He wants to know what's taking us so long."

And just that easy, I forgot all about what we'd been talking about. Standing up, I held my hand out for her. "Come on. You sneak down first. I'll have your back. James Bond has nothing on me."

CHAPTER TWO

I didn't hear from PA the rest of the weekend. Monday morning I was still flying high from the party Friday night with Alexandra Maple and her killer legs that I had a feeling she showed off that night just for me. As I pulled myself out of bed for the last week of school before three months of freedom, I hit the power button on my computer to let it warm up while I showered. Not that I expected her to get back to me. If she waited this long, she'd probably punked out. Which sucked for the wallet, but I didn't really want to work with someone who wasn't sure anyway.

With my hair still wet and dripping on the collar of my shirt, I sat down at my desk and fired up my Hook-up Doctor account. One new message. "Hell, yeah."

Dear Know-it-All,

Well, looked like I'd lost my "Mr." title already.

14

Okay, I don't know who you think you are, but you know nothing about me. I happen to know exactly who I am! You can't blame me for being a little nervous. I mean, you're not even willing to let anyone know who you are, so obviously that tells me you're not as confident about this whole thing as you want everyone to believe. Hmmm? Could I be right?

I stifled a laugh. This chick didn't play around.

That being said, I'm willing to give you a try. Just like a guy needs money, a girl could use a little help. You were right about the whole double-standard-thing. I figure I'll take all the help I can get.

So, about me. I DO know who I am. I'm the friend. I'm not shy, but I'm not real forward when it comes to guys either. I've um . . . well, not really had a lot of experience. I mean, I had a boyfriend for a couple weeks once, and I've played my fair share of spin the bottle, but I've never really done the dating thing. I've definitely never done the seducing-a-guy thing. I'm your basic girl.

15

I do well in school. I have friends, play sports and all that stuff. I'm not one of those girls who wear shirts two sizes too small so guys stare at their breasts.

THE GUY (I can't think of a name) is the kind of guy who goes for those girls wearing shirts two sizes too small. He's not really a relationship kind of guy. Well, let me rephrase that. I think he would be, if he found the right girl. I know him, and I know there's more to him than he shows everyone. He's funny and sarcastic. Umm, likes music. Everyone loves him. He's one of those guys who has a ton of friends, but he doesn't realize how much people like him. Deep down, he's a really good guy.

"Sounds like you got yourself a chump," I said to my computer. What was it with girls? He has a ton of friends, but he doesn't realize how much people like him. Yeah right. He realizes it, he just doesn't want you to know he does. It was all about how you played the game, and it sounded like her chump knew how to play.

Even more important than her "he's-sensitive-on-the-inside" issue was the fact that she was blind. She tried to see something in this guy that wasn't there. I'd seen the mistake made a million times. My mom had made it a million times herself. If you have to use the words, "deep down" all that means is you're fooling yourself. You're seeing what you want to see and not what's really there.

But she wasn't paying me to tell her that. Not that she'd paid me anything yet, but when she did, she'd be paying me to hook her up, not tell her that even though she'd get the guy, it wouldn't last. It never did, and I wasn't just talking about the people I hooked-up, either.

A honk sounded from outside. I closed down my email, picked up my backpack and ran for the stairs. Jaden sat outside in his beatermobile that had about ten different colors of paint on it. I used to give him shit about it until he pointed out that a piece of crap was better than no car at all. So now I sucked it up and rode with him to school every day. I could always ride with Aspen. Her car's a lot nicer. One of those electric things that she has to plug in every once in a while, but she picked up Pris every day. It made no sense because Priscilla had her own car. Whatever. Girls were weird that way. Anyway, I don't like to get up any earlier than I had to, so Jay and the beatermobile it was.

17

"What's up?" I asked, wincing as the door creaked and stuck when I tried to pull it closed.

"Yeah, it's doing that now. Gotta pull hard, Rambo." Jaden scratched his bleached hair as I jerked the door closed. "There ya go. I knew you had it in you," he said, sarcasm dripped from his words. "You ride in my car enough, you could help me work on it, you know."

"Whatever. I'm too pretty to work on cars," I teased him.

He rolled his eyes at me and backed out of my driveway before he started for the school. "So, Alexandra . . . Hot, huh?" he leaned back in his seat, one hand on the stick-shift and the other on the wheel.

"Yep," was all I said. I didn't do the whole kiss and tell thing. What I did was my business. Well, and the girl's. I hadn't kissed her too much, anyway. I planned on rectifying that soon.

Jay didn't ask anything else, because he knew I wouldn't tell. We were at school about ten minutes later. As I closed his ghetto door, the bell rang. Perfect timing. "See ya later, man," I called out to him. While jogging to my locker, I looked around, but didn't see Pris or Aspen, so I headed straight to class. I didn't pay much attention all morning, trying to formulate a plan for my little do-gooder who obviously had it in her head to save a sap. Ha. Save a sap. I could use that one again.

By the time lunch rolled around, I had a rough game plan set out for her. I met Jaden, Aspen and Pris by our table under a tree. Pris's long, black hair was curly today. It was crazy how she did that. Some days it would be straight as a board, and others it looked like my Grandma's poodle, only longer. Of course, I never told her that. Pris would start yelling in Spanish at me, and then proceed to try and kick my ass. She rocked, though. Pris and Aspen were both cool girls.

"Hey, ladies." I walked up and put my arm around Aspen's shoulder. She bumped me with her hip before mumbling a "what's up".

"What? You can't say hi to me? See if I give you any more rides to school." Jaden jumped on the picnic table, much more awake than he'd been this morning.

"There's only four more days. I don't need any more rides. Plus, I did say hi to you."

"No, you said—" his eyes widened. "You don't have to make excuses for thinking I'm pretty. I won't tell anyone you swing that way." We all laughed.

"Boys are so weird. I really don't understand how

their brains work," Aspen mumbled to Pris before pulling away from me.

"That's because girls think too much."

Pris shook her head at me while Aspen's eyes bugged out of her head like I'd said something that surprised her. Just as quickly as the look flashed on her face, it was gone. The three of us walked over to the table, and sat down with Jaden. The sun beat down on me, making little beads of perspiration cling to my forehead, teasing of the summer that sat right around the corner.

"I can't wait to be out of this place for three months." I grabbed a chip out of Pris's bag and popped it into my mouth.

"Why? Aren't you going to spend the summer slaving away at some minimum wage job so you can save cash for your car? I think you need to skip the whole job thing, Bastian. It's summer. It's a time for lakes, parties and girls in bikinis." He held up his hand, and I didn't leave him hanging. "Plus, I have the car. Mi beater es su beater."

Pris threw her apple at him, which Jaden caught and bit into. She narrowed her eyes at him. "Usted es un idiota."

We didn't study many insults in Spanish class, but I was pretty sure she just called Jaden an idiot.

20

Jay took another bite, and then spoke around the food in his mouth. "I have no idea what you just said, but thanks for the apple."

. I laughed, before moving down to the bench seat on the same side of the table as Jaden. He continued to munch on the apple. I ignored him and looked at Pris and Aspen because they were much better at solving problems than Jay was. "Despite the offer to share Jaden's POS, I want my own wheels. Woodstock, can you hook me up with a job at the hippie shop?"

She smiled at me, not at all bothered by my teasing. I'd known these guys my whole life; we were cool to give each other a hard time without anyone getting their feelings hurt. That was what I loved about them. "I can't. The economy sucks right now. My parents can't afford to pay anyone. Sorry, Bastian."

"Maybe if you got a haircut, someone would hire you? You're looking a little shaggy these days." Pris put her elbows up on the table.

I ruffled my wavy, black hair. "I happen to like my hair."

She shrugged. "It's your summer shacked up in the beatermobile. Not mine."

"Can't you hook me up with a job at the mall? Put in a good word with your boss or something?" I asked her. The money I brought in as The Hook-up Doctor was good, but it wasn't enough. I figured with both gigs, I'd have a car in no time. I tried the lip-poking-out-thing like my mom did.

"Sebastian, I work at a girl's clothing store, remember? You're not metro-sexual enough to work there."

I raised my eyebrows. "No, I didn't remember, because you still haven't hooked me up with one of the hot girls who work there."

"You're such a cerdo." She turned to face Aspen and they started girl talking about clothes and that British guy who sparkled in all those vampire movies. Jay turned and plopped down beside me, tossing Pris's apple core into her bag. We did study animals, and I totally disagreed with her. I wasn't a pig. I just happened to like girls. A lot.

"Are you still holding out on me about the party?" Jaden asked.

I rolled my eyes. "I don't ask you about your hook-ups. Don't ask me about mine." This time, it was only partly because I didn't care. The other part was because I already knew. Alex told me her friend Dana had it bad for Jay. I'd seen them talking and hanging all over each other at the party. Another lesson I could give PA. Two plus two always made four. Talking at a party, plus a crush equaled some kind of hook-up. Or at least the prospect of one.

"Yeah, but—" Jaden started, but stopped when a high-pitched voice cut him off.

"Hey, Jaden. Sebastian." Speak of the she-devils. Dana with her short blond hair and Alex with her even shorter skirt stood beside us. Dana played with her hair as she spoke.

"Hey," I glanced up, trying not to take in the sight too long, knowing if I acted disinterested, it would make them all the more interested in me. I know that makes me sound like a jerk, and maybe in some ways I am, but girls play games, too. Guys are just more likely to admit to it. It wasn't as if I was playing any games with them that they wouldn't play with me. I know girls. An act like this wouldn't work with all of them, and there's a group of ladies out there I wouldn't even try it with. Girls like Dana and Alex though . . . they liked the chase just as much as I did. There was nothing wrong with that.

Plus, the girls I went for always knew the score up front. I never pretended to want anything long term, because, even though I enjoyed the chase, okay and the capture too, I would never hurt someone the way my mom had been hurt. I'd picked up the pieces too many times to do that to someone else.

"What's up?" Jaden gave them a little wave, acting

the same as me. We'd done this enough together to know how it worked.

"I had fun with you at the party, Seb." Alex winked at me, and I cringed. Seb? I shouldn't even have to mention that's a lame nickname. Turns out, I didn't. As I opened my mouth to speak, Aspen cut me off.

"He hates that nickname."

I smiled at her. She hated these girls, but I knew she told Alex for my benefit, just as much as she did to stick it to her.

"I'm sorry, Denver. I didn't realize I was talking to you. Why don't you go back to being the 'friend'? Don't blame me that you're stuck there because you didn't have the guts to go for it. The jealous look is never attractive."

My whole body tensed at her words. Across from me, Pris pushed to her feet. "Back-off, Barbie. Don't talk to my friend that way." Aspen stood up, too.

"Pris, chill." She narrowed her eyes at me, and then sat back down. I shot a glance at Jaden, and he nodded his head. I knew he'd agree with me. Our friends came before getting some. "Listen, I know we hung out this weekend, but that doesn't give you the right to talk shit to my girls." I crossed my arms. "I'm not trying to be a prick to you either, but if we're going to hang out, you can't treat them like crap."

I was stuck between two walls of estrogen: Pris and Aspen on one side who wanted me to kick these girls to the curb so fast their heads knocked together, and Alex and Dana who I couldn't completely blow off because I did have my tongue down Alex's throat this weekend. I didn't do the dating thing, but I wasn't a total ass, either.

"Why don't you call me tonight?" I told her, hoping to get her to go away before Pris killed them. She gave me a sassy little wink and ran her hand through my hair. Yeah, this definitely wasn't going to last long. I hated it when girls played with my hair.

"Okay. You can come over if you want. My parents won't be home." She grabbed Dana's hand as Dana said goodbye to Jaden and pulled her away.

Jay's head whipped toward me, his smile saying the same thoughts that ran through my head. No parents? What guy could pass up that opportunity?

"Do you even like them?" Aspen asked.

I turned toward her and gave her one of my best smiles. "She's hot, Woodstock."

Aspen flipped me off and stood up. "You guys suck." She turned to Pris. "Come on. Let's go."

Jaden and I started laughing as they walked off. "Come on. You know you guys love us!" I yelled after them.

They didn't turn around, and after our laughter died, Jaden spoke. "Aspen's got a nice ass. When did that happen?"

I don't know why, but I nudged Jaden hard with my shoulder. Apparently, hard enough to make him fall backward. "What the hell?" he asked.

I shook my head. What the hell was right. "Nothin'," I told him, a little surprised myself that it annoyed me when he brought up Aspen's butt. "Come on. If we hurry, we might be able to catch up with Alex and Dana before lunch is over."

"Are you writing love letters over there or what?" Jaden tapped his hands on the steering wheel to the beat of a song playing. I didn't know who the band was. Some pop crap I didn't listen to. We were on our way to Alex's. We *had* managed to catch up with them after the girls took off. After a little more digging, we'd found out her parents were going to be out at least until midnight. We made plans for dinner, which Jaden and I picked up on our way and then to watch a movie I had no intention of watching.

Watching a movie was code for making out.

The dinner cost me twenty bucks from my car funds so, yeah, I was messaging my client on the way. "To your mama."

"Dude, you're so lame."

"Whatever." I finished my email to PA with directions on how and when to drop the money off and hit send. "This summer needs to be epic. Seriously, man. We need to come up with some sort of plan or something. I'm tired of the same old thing." Though I couldn't wait for summer to begin, I knew exactly what it would be. Sitting around town, working, hanging with the girls, parties and Mom's new man.

My attempt to change the subject worked. "Did you know Pris's parents are renting her a beach house for her birthday? It's supposed to be some girl-fest thing with her and Aspen, but damn, that would be tight if we could go. Beach chicks, no parents. Think you can work it? Talk to Aspen and get her to put a word in with Pris or something?"

I played with my eyebrow ring like I always did when thinking. "Why me?"

"Because you guys are like BFFs or something. I think you're secretly in love. Oh, maybe you'll run off to some hippie commune together one day!"

My friend was an idiot. "You need serious help. First of all, I might be a little closer to Woodstock, but that's only because we've lived down the street from each other forever. I had to drink my first cup of soy milk with her. People bond over that shit."

27

Jaden laughed.

"Second, we're not secretly in love. I'm not even sure she's into guys. She's had, like, one boyfriend or something. Even if she is, I do hook-ups, not love. Aspen wouldn't be down for that. But since Pris wishes you would die a fiery death, I'm sure you're right. I can probably score us an invite way before you can. Plus, I just have better skills than you do."

About that time we pulled onto Alex's street. Six o'clock on the dot. Damn, we were good. Jay parked a block away, just to be on the safe side. Escaping the parentals was always easier if you didn't run the risk of getting blocked into their driveway.

"I'm going to let that go because we're here, and I definitely think it would put a damper on our night if I kicked your ass." Jaden snickered as he got out and slammed the door. Slipping my phone in the pocket of my baggy, low-slung shorts, I was right behind him. He had the drinks in his hands, and I had bags of burgers and fries in mine.

Alex opened the door before we had the chance to knock. I took in the view. Short skirt, tight shirt, her hand on her waist with the sassy, I am woman look. Nice.

"Come on in." She held the door open, closing

28

it when Jaden and I walked inside. Dana stood behind her.

"How you doin'?" Jaden asked, his voice all funny like he was trying to be cool. I held in my laugh. I'd have to give him some pointers on that.

Alex led the way up to her room, shaking her butt as she went.

See? That was a nice butt. What had Jaden been talking about earlier when he commented on Aspen's? She didn't have near the curves as Alex did. Woodstock's was smaller . . . tighter . . . *Whoa?* Had I been checking out Aspen's ass, too? I mean, I noticed the sliver of skin. When had I started noticing the rest of her?

Jaden closed the bedroom door behind us. I squinted at the bright burst of yellow that jumped out at me. "Wow . . ."

"What can I say? Just call me Little Miss Sunshine," Alex purred. A floral scent itched my nose when she stepped closer to me. The girl was lucky she had a nice butt.

Dana and Jaden curled up on the couch in Alex's room. She was one of those rich kids like Pris where Daddy went all out for her. With Pris, you'd never know it. She didn't flaunt that her parents had more money than Bill Gates.

Alex's room had to be about three of mine. It looked

29

like a small apartment and had a flat screen on the wall. After grabbing two sodas from Jay, I climbed onto the bed. I patted the spot beside me. "Sit with me?" I asked.

She did just that. We ate our food and talked about the upcoming summer. Before I knew it, the movie was on and the lights were down.

I know it might seem like it, but I'm not a jerk. I usually gave a girl at least thirty minutes into the movie before I tried anything. It's the adjustment period, where I really got a feel for what she wanted. Is she sitting close to me? Leaning toward me? Was her hand strategically placed between us for me to hold? All those are signs, little beacons that let me know if there will be anything more or not. I never moved forward unless I was absolutely sure.

With Alex, I didn't have to wait. As soon as we finished eating, her slinky little hand slid up my leg and every radar in my body beamed. *Hell yes! Houston, we have the green light!*

Before I knew it, the credits were rolling. I had no idea what the movie had been about, my jaw hurt, and I had my hand on the curvy backside I'd been admiring earlier. It's a wonder I heard the noise at all, but like I said, my damn jaw hurt from the marathon kiss session. Not that I was complaining, but it was starting to cramp up.

"Princess?" The closed door didn't do enough to muffle the very dad-like voice on the other side.

"Oh shit!" Jaden said from the couch. I jerked away from Alex. A little too far, because I tumbled off the side of the bed, making a loud thump.

"Shh," I loudly shushed Jaden like Alex's dad didn't already hear his curse and my fall.

"Alexandra!" The door rattled. Someone had been smart enough to lock it. I scrambled to my feet. My sore jaw was nothing compared to my heart trying to jump out of my chest. Jaden's wide eyes scanned the room, obviously as freaked as I was. I don't know what he had to worry about. He was only kissing the friend. I'm the one who had my hand up his princess's skirt.

Alex and Dana started pacing the room.

It was only 8:30. "I thought you said they weren't coming home till midnight!" I don't know why it mattered to me. They were here and we were dead unless we could get out of there.

"Hold on, Daddy! I'm getting dressed," she replied.

I hit my forehead with the palm of my hand. Lying wasn't going to work at this point, and if she was going to lie, getting dressed was probably the dumbest one she could come up with.

A loud crash sounded from the hallway. "Alexandra, you open this door right now!"

I ran for the window and pulled it open. Thank God for trees. "Come on, Jay!" I crawled onto the branch, hoping like hell the thing wouldn't snap.

"Hurry!" Jaden practically pushed me out of the way to join me. As soon as he did, I heard a crack. Fumbling my way toward the trunk of the tree, I wrapped my arms around it like it had been Alex about five minutes ago. Jaden latched on behind me, his arms round me, too.

"Get off!" I pushed at him as he wormed his way beside me. We started scaling down.

"You little punks!" I looked up to see Alex's red-faced dad sticking out of the window. "I'm going to castrate you!"

No way could I lose it before I really had the chance to use it. My hands stung as I slid down the tree. The second Jaden and I hit the ground, I saw her front door jerk open. Daddy was pissed and he *had* a bat! We ran. Unfortunately, Jaden's car was the opposite direction. My chest hurt, but I pushed forward, Jaden right beside me. Daddy was on our tail, swinging his bat and cursing.

"Pris!" I told him. She lived in this neighborhood. We cut through a yard, picking up speed trying to lose him. As we hit the next street over, I saw them. Pris and Aspen stood in Pris's driveway. They were looking at something in the trunk of Aspen's car. A quick glance behind me told me we might have lost him. I wasn't going to take any chances.

I looked again. He hadn't rounded the corner yet. I had no choice but to dive in the trunk. Jaden was right behind me.

"Where'd you go you little punks?" He was still after us. Aspen must have put two and two together pretty quickly and slammed the trunk. She always was smart.

As I fought to catch my breath, Jaden's sweaty back against mine, I cursed. The girls were never going to let us live this down.

CHAPTER THREE

Hook-up Doctor,

Did you get the money? Don't blame me if someone took it. That was your fifty bucks, and you're not getting any more until the job is done. Sorry I was a little late dropping it off. I had an . . . issue. Anyway, hope you got it, and I'm ready to hear what to do next. I have my doubts, but yeah, I'm still here, so I guess that means there's something wrong with me. LOL. Hmm, maybe I should have asked for references? What makes you such an expert, Mr. Hook-up Doctor?

PA

PA,

I'm the best. I can promise you that. You want Mr. Deep on the Inside, and you'll get him. Anyway, yeah, I got the money. I had an issue myself, so I was late, too. No biggie.

Issue was putting it mildly. Jaden and I were too freaked out to risk stopping by Alex's house for the beatermobile right away. I'd had all sorts of visions of her scary, psycho dad waiting to jump out of the car and make good on his castration promise. It was like one of those *Saw* movies, complete with crazy masks and tying me up in the basement.

But then that had created another problem, because I needed to pick up the money. It was easy to make up some lame excuse to Jaden as to why I'd need a few minutes alone in the park by myself, because, well, because he wouldn't give a shit. The girls were a different thing. I'd known they would want all the details on what I'd be doing; want to know why they had to wait in the car, and there'd been no way I could use meeting a girl as an excuse, because they would have locked me in the trunk again and never let me out. After the period of time they'd already kept us in there. Nice, huh?

No matter how many excuses I'd come up with, they'd shot them down, countering with excuses of their own. Finally, we'd risked Alex's dad's wrath by getting dropped off at the car, where I'd then had to let Jaden drop me off at home and walk back to the park by myself. So yeah, I got the issues thing.

Right now, that wasn't as important as getting back to my email though. I'd pout about it later. Where had I been? Oh yeah, references.

As for references, that would be against my privacy policy. But I've never had problems getting girls when I want them ;).

Your first step is an easy one: pay a lot of attention to him. I know you're going to think it's lame, but trust the Doctor. You do this, and he'll feel the next step even more. We're guys; we love attention, so you can never go wrong with it. And with us, you always gotta start out slow. Be nice, friendly, helpful, the whole nine yards. Since you're friends, it shouldn't be too hard, but step it up a notch, k? He needs to notice the difference.

I'll be in touch.

Hook-up Doctor.

"Are you sure you don't want to ride in the trunk?" Aspen laughed from the driver's seat of her car. It had been a week since what I liked to refer to as "the incident," but she still wasn't letting it go.

"Ha, ha. I'm still mad you and Pris thought it would be fun to drive around town for ten hours before letting us out." I closed the door behind me and clicked my seatbelt in.

Aspen flipped her hair over her shoulder. It looked all shiny and flowy, which was pretty strange since she usually wore it up. "You're such a baby. It was like, thirty minutes not ten hours."

"Humph. Try being in that small of a space with Jaden and tell me it doesn't feel like a lifetime. I'm still having nightmares about it."

"That was karma's way of telling you to steer clear of Alex the tramp. God, I can't believe you even went over there. And then you wanted to go meet someone else at the park! You didn't say it, but don't think we didn't know that's what you wanted. You're such a perv." Aspen kept her eyes on the road as she drove.

I decided to ignore the park comment. I wasn't in the mood to go there again. "No, I'm a guy, and she's a hot chick. Any guy would have done the same thing for you."

As soon as the words left my mouth Aspen's head whirled around to look at me, and I realized what I just said. Did I just call Aspen, my friend since I was like—I don't know, an embryo or something, a hot chick? *Wow* . . . "I didn't mean that how it sounded." When her face got all squished up, I realized I'd just screwed up again. "Not that I don't think you're hot,

I just don't think you're *hot*. You know, you're like friend hot, not let's make-out hot."

"What?" Her voice was tight, and I realized I kept digging myself deeper and deeper, but I couldn't seem to stop.

"Come on, Woodstock. You know what I mean. You're the friend. There's nothing wrong with being in the friend territory." I felt like jumping out of the car and letting her run me over. I'd just used Alex's words on her. What was wrong with me? I didn't want to insult the girl.

She shook her head. "Whatever, Bastian. You're lucky I'm such a good friend."

I was, because apparently, I sucked at the friendship thing today.

I nudged her arm, trying to change the subject. "Thanks for taking me job hunting today. Pretty soon I'll get a job, then I'll have wheels and you won't ever have to worry about lugging me around in your trunk again." See? I could make fun of myself when it counted.

She laughed, and I knew I was off the hook. "You know I'd do anything for you, Sebastian. I don't know why, but I would."

Her reply made me say, "That's because we're BFFs. Jaden told me that last week."

Aspen tucked a wayward strand of her hair behind her ear. "It's because I know you're a good guy. Buried deep—deep under that teenage boy exterior, you, Sebastian Hawkins, are a sweetheart. I know it's hard to believe, but I wouldn't be such good friends with you otherwise."

I gulped, almost swallowing my tongue. Aspen's words were eerily familiar. It was like she'd copied them out of PA's email. Hell, from what she said, not only could she be PA, but I could be the chump! It couldn't be, could it? No. Aspen was not the kind of girl to email someone about hooking up with a guy, and I sure wasn't a chump.

"Did I mention it's really, *really* under the surface? Like practically microscopic?"

I laughed, wiping out all the thoughts from before. This was my friend, that's all, and we both knew it. "Please. I like, exude sweetness."

She patted my leg and then put her hand back on the wheel. Relaxed, I dropped my head against the seat to take a little nap before I had to fill out my first application.

"A-spen. We filled out like a million applications today, plus the ones I did online. Everyone looked at me like they were going to toss them in the trash when I walked out. I'm done. This is lame. Let's go do something fun." I put my feet up on the dashboard of her car. One narrow-eyed look from Aspen later, I put them back on the floor.

"You're never going to get a job with that attitude. Do you want to be stuck in the beatermobile for the rest of your life?"

"Jaden's beater es my beater." I shook my head. "Or something like that. I suck at Spanish." This wasn't how I wanted to spend the beginning of my summer. I needed a job. I needed money, but we'd been at it for hours, and I was done. My hand was practically cramped closed, and I doubt Aspen wanted to spend her day doing this, either.

"You know, I'm not even the one who needs a job, and I've wasted my whole day out here with you, and you don't hear me complaining," she said.

I was totally a mind reader, but she was right. I was whining. It was pretty cool of her to do this for me, but I was still done. "You're the best. We all know that, Woodstock. I'm not giving up. Just done for today."

"Whatever. Your loss. I need to run by the restaurant and get my schedule though."

Ugh. How could I have forgotten she had a job, too? Probably because she didn't work much during the school year, but now it made me feel like an even bigger loser.

My stomach growled, which trumped my whining. "Will they give us free pizza?"

Her only response was to roll her eyes at me. A few minutes later we walked into the dive she worked in. "Hey! Look who it is. It's our Rocky Mountain Girl!" some guy yelled from behind the counter. There was another dude and two girls back there that looked up smiling and said hi to Aspen. A strange pinch twinged inside me. Rocky Mountain girl? Who were these people, and when had they gotten a nickname for my friend? Couldn't they get any more creative than that?

"Hey guys!" Aspen smiled and walked behind the counter, leaving me. It felt weird being on the opposite side as her. We were always together. A group. A package deal, or whatever.

I watched as she hugged the girls, gave one guy a high five, then turned to the last guy and smiled at him.

"You going to introduce me to your friends, Woodstock?" I leaned over the counter.

"This is Matt," she pointed to the smiley guy in the back, the one who she'd grinned at, and I felt the strange urge to punch him in the face. "Bradley, Liz, and Sara." After giving me all their names, she pointed at me. "This is my friend, Sebastian."

"Best friend," I blurted out and then wanted to punch myself in the face for sounding so dumb. At this rate, I'd be painting nails with her any day now. Thank God, Jaden wasn't here.

Aspen's eyes squished up as she looked at me. "Um, yeah. My best friend." She leaned against the counter from the other side. "How's it been today?" she asked them.

They started blabbing about how busy it had been, but the place looked pretty dead to me. I stood back watching her talk to them and wondered why I hadn't realized she had this whole other life outside of me. Not like I thought I was her life or anything, but it was always me, Woodstock, Jaden and Pris. We hung out together, partied together. Now there was a group of people who thought Woodstock was their little "Rocky Mountain Girl," and it kind of annoyed me. Which made me sound like an ass, but it was just because I cared about her. *Them.* I cared about them. I'd be the same way if it was Pris. They were my girls, and I just wanted to make sure no one would mess with them. As long as I knew these guys were cool, I'd be cool.

See? Aren't I a good friend?

"Crap! DJ's here. Get on the other side of the counter. You don't have your uniform on." One of her new friends rushed her away.

I felt my lips curl up into a smile as Aspen ran back around the counter and stood next to me. I stood behind her and wrapped my arms around her shoulders with my chin resting on top of her head. It wasn't unusual. I touched her like this a lot, but I felt her squirm a little bit, but then she leaned back into me and I relaxed, figuring I imagined it.

"Hi, Rocky." Some guy, I assumed it was DJ, said as he came inside. What the hell was it with the nickname? They acted like they'd known Aspen her whole life instead of a few weeks.

"Hey, DJ. I just came in to check my schedule." She stepped away from me.

The red headed guy handed her a piece of paper. "Here, I have a copy right here. I've been busting my ass trying to fill in the holes. Trish quit with no notice, so we need to get someone else hired pretty quick."

The homing beacon inside me I usually used to find girls started beeping. I stepped forward and held out my hand. "Hi. I'm Aspen's friend, Sebastian. I'd love to fill out an application."

Thirty minutes later, I had my app filled out and had pretty much been promised the job. A pizza place definitely wasn't my dream job, but it paid, and Aspen worked there, so it couldn't be that bad. We were almost to our houses where she was going to get dressed and then head back to DJ's. The cocky-smile guy had mentioned something about needing the evening off, and Aspen had jumped at the opportunity to work for him.

When she pulled into her driveway, I turned to her. "So. The people you work with? They're cool?" I felt all proud of myself for wanting to protect my friend.

"Yep. You'll like them. Bradley's a shift leader. He's pretty kick back. Liz is a delivery driver, so she's in and out a lot. Matt started about the same time as I did. You'll like him. He reminds me of you, actually. I've gotten to know him pretty well."

I tried not to roll my eyes. "Pfft. He looked like a loser to me. All Smiley Mcsmilerson. I think you need to watch your back around him. I got a funny feeling about him."

"What? You talked to him for like two seconds. He's a good guy. Real funny." She poked me in the side. "Much like you, Bastian." With that, she climbed out of the car. I pushed the door open and jogged over to her.

"Wanna hang out Friday night? We can see what

44

Pris and Jaden are up to." The words tumbled out of my mouth without a thought.

Aspen shrugged. "Sure. I get off at six, so we can do something after that. I gotta go though. I need to get into work."

Before she walked away, I grabbed her and hugged her, the whole time thinking I was being pretty damn cheesy right now. It wasn't like we never hugged, but usually she was doing the hugging, and I was doing the hugging back. Aspen must have noticed because she laughed against me. "Bastian, you're being weird. Is everything okay?"

When our hug ended, I ruffled her hair, because I was being weird, and it started to freak me out. "I'm cool."

"How's your mom? She still seeing that guy?" Her mouth turned down, and her eyes got all soft.

I sure didn't want to talk about that, even with Aspen. She was the only one who knew how much my mom's boyfriends pissed me off, but still, I wasn't one to sit around and harp on it. My shoulders lifted into a shrug. "Beats me." I playfully pushed her toward the door. "Now get in there and get ready for work before you're late. I don't want it to look bad on me, now that you're my reference and all."

Aspen laughed. "Bye, Bastian."

"Bye." As she walked away, I found myself watching her. Jaden was right. While we weren't looking, Aspen did get a nice butt.

And I needed to get myself an appointment with my mom's shrink, because there was definitely something wrong with me.

CHAPTER FOUR

PA,

Hey. Hope you got a chance to see lover boy and give him some quality time ;). I'm going to go ahead and give you your next step now. If you haven't had a chance to do the first one, get on it girl. What are you waiting for? Dream Man won't be around forever. Gotta be proactive and all that crap.

So, now that you were all nice and helpful to him, it's time to take a step back. A few actually. I know it's hard, but you have to pretty much ignore him. Don't be bitchy, because that's going to make him run for the hills, but show him you have a life without him. Go out. Have fun. Talk about it so he hears you—or better yet, let him see you out.

He knows what it's like to have you there for him, and he'll miss you all the more when you're not. Let me know how it's going.

Hook-up Doctor

"Sebastian. Time to get up. We're meeting Roger for lunch in an hour." I'd originally planned on playing possum, but as soon as she muttered the words Roger and lunch, my eyes shot open to see Mom standing in the doorway of my bedroom. She had on a tight-fitting shirt and a skirt. I recognized it as one of her favorite date outfits. It was one of the ones she wore when she really wanted to impress. Shit.

"Ma, you can't spring something like this on me. I'm half asleep. I need to make a good impression when I meet him." My mouth felt all cottony, like I had to pry my lips apart to speak. My heart beat a little too fast for having just woken up.

Mom sighed and her voice came out all soft. "You don't want to meet him, do you?"

My shell started to crumble. I didn't like hurting my mom. No, I hated hurting her. She'd been hurt enough that she shouldn't have to get it from her own son, too. We were all each other had. "Ma."

"No, no. It's okay. I understand. I really wish you'd change your mind though. He's important to me, but you're more important. I won't make you do something you don't want to do."

She moved to close the door. "No!" I called out, stopping her. I wanted nothing to do with this guy, but I wasn't willing to hurt my mom over it. "I'll go.

I just need to call Jaden and cancel my plans. It's not a big deal."

Her face lit up. It was always so easy to make her happy. I wondered if that was the reason so many guys had been "the one" for her, and why it had been so hard for them to keep making her feel that way. She didn't ask for much, but none of them had ever been willing to keep giving it to her.

"Are you sure?"

"Hell yeah. I haven't had the chance to give him the warning speech. He needs to know if he hurts my mom, he'll have to deal with me."

I pushed out of bed, running a hand through my messy hair. The smile on her face made it worth it.

"I love you, kiddo. I don't know how I got so lucky."

She closed the door before I mumbled, "I love you, too."

So, Roger pretty much looked like a loser. He was one of those suit and tie guys with a comb-over. She'd never, ever dated a guy with a comb-over before. She usually liked musicians or guys who were in motorcycle clubs. If this guy was in high school, he'd be in the math club.

I still didn't like him.

He held my mom's hand through most of the meal.

If you ask me, that seemed pretty awkward. The whole time I wanted to yell at him, "Sometimes it takes two hands to eat, buddy, give her some space." Plus, it always felt like showboating to me, trying to brand a girl as yours. Lame. I'd never wanted to brand a girl, and I hated that he was doing it to my mom. But of course, I didn't say anything. I was the perfect gentleman, because I knew it would upset Mom if I wasn't.

He talked through most of the meal. He was divorced. An accountant, which made me laugh. Definitely the math club.

He also owned a house. Liked watching my mom dance—too much information for me. Yeah, it wasn't skeezy dancing, but still. He kept going on and on, yada, yada, until I wanted to tape his mouth shut.

Then the conversation turned to me. "How do you like school, Sebastian?" Roger asked me after he finished his salad. *Salad*! What kind of guy orders a fuckin' salad for lunch?

"It's summer."

"Sebastian . . ." Mom kind of coughed at me.

"Oh! I forgot about that. Well, how do you like school when it's in?" He gave me a smile.

I didn't feel like talking, but knew I didn't have a choice. "It's okay. As cool as school can be, I guess."

I started playing with my eyebrow ring, hoping he'd stop talking to me, but he didn't.

"So, you said summer break then? You'll be a senior next year, right?" The loser let go of my mom's hand, but started tickling the top of it. It was weird to watch. I couldn't stop focusing on their hands. I'd never really seen her like this with someone before.

"Yep."

"Do you know what you plan to do after?"

Hell, I hated this question. Why was it always the first one people asked? It's like parents thought your whole life depended on this one answer. Made no sense to me, even though I kind of did know the answer to it. "Not for sure. My friends and I want to take a road trip next summer. Aspen and Pris are planning on going to college in New York. I think Jay and I are going to tag along."

My mom cut in, reaching across the table to pat my hand. "Don't let Sebastian fool you. He's into music. The boy can pick up almost any instrument and play it. He's already got pamphlets in his room for some fancy music school out there."

I pulled my hand back and sighed. "Ma, I was just looking. I don't even know if I want to go to school right away." I picked up another fry and popped it in my mouth, even though I wasn't really hungry. "It's hard as hell to get into. They probably wouldn't take me anyway."

"Language, Sebastian."

My eyes snapped up to hers. "Sorry," I mumbled. I hated it when she tried to make us look like some perfect family. Yeah, I was pretty damn good at music. I played guitar and piano (most of my friends didn't know the piano part), but a career in music was pretty much like wanting to be an actor or something. It didn't happen often. Plus, I had time to figure all that out. I sure didn't plan on stressing about it now.

And the language thing. I couldn't remember the last time she gave me a hard time for saying hell. But then, I knew she just wanted to make a good impression. She was obviously head over heels for the guy. Why, I didn't know.

"It's okay." She stood. "Now, if you boys would excuse me for a minute, I need to go to the restroom."

Great. Just what I didn't want: to be left alone with math club. I focused on my half dead food so I didn't have to look at him. I didn't trust myself not to say something I shouldn't, not to find a way to ruin this for her. Honestly, what I really wanted to do is tell the guy to stay the hell away from us. But would I really be ruining it for her or saving her in the long run? I didn't know, and I wasn't willing to risk finding out.

After a minute or two of silence, Roger broke it. "Can I talk to you man to man for a minute, Sebastian?" he asked.

This was the perfect opening for me. I leaned back in the chair and crossed my arms. "As long as I can do the same with you."

He nodded his head, with a partial smile on his face. "Fair enough. You go first."

"My mom means everything to me. She's been through a lot, and the last thing she needs is another jerk that's going to bail on her. I don't want to see her hurt again, so if you're playing games, play them with someone else." A deep breath escaped my lungs. This was the thing, what all those girls who emailed me to hook them up didn't understand. Getting a guy isn't the same thing as keeping him. I can always promise a hook-up, but I can't control if it lasts or not. As far as I could tell, it almost never lasted.

If you asked me, I wasn't sure it was worth the risk.

The putz looked at me and smiled. "Your mom is very lucky to have you for a son, Sebastian."

"I know." I hated to sound cocky, but I knew I was a pretty good son. Despite everything, she was a good mom, too. The jury was still out on this guy. Guilty until proven innocent when it came to her.

Roger took a drink of his water. "I wanted to let you know, I'm in love with your mom. She's a special woman. If I have your permission, I'd like to ask her to be my wife."

The fries and burger churned in my stomach. They'd been dating like six weeks, and he wanted to marry her? Hell, the ones she'd tied herself to with that stupid piece of paper had turned out to be the biggest assholes. My dad included. And for her, when it fell apart, she always felt like she failed even more than if they just broke up. Like that piece of paper made everything so much more of a big deal.

Roger must have been able to read the look on my face. Or heard my breathing pick up. For all I knew, he heard how hard my heart pounded, because he said, "I know it's quick, but there is something about her. She's genuine. I've been alone a long time, and this is the first time I've been willing to make this step again."

His speech was nice, but I still wasn't sure. It sounded like a politician's speech, and even I knew how those usually turned out. Before I could tell the guy, hell no, my mom came back to the table and sat down. Knowing myself, I probably wouldn't have said no anyway. Not if there was a chance it could make her happy. Was that a good thing or a bad thing? I didn't know.

Unaware of what just went down, of what he said and how I wanted to explode, Mom smiled. "So! What did I miss?"

I opened my mouth, but Roger cut me off. "Just a little guy talk. It can wait."

Sitting there, watching her smile at him, her big heart plastered on her forehead, I knew I was screwed. My mom loved the guy. There's no way I could tell him no and be the one to break her heart. Hopefully, he'd give this some time. You know, sleep on it for more than five minutes. All I knew was, if he hurt her, he'd better pray he never ran into me again.

I blew the head off a video game zombie. A second later, I sniped another one and then another. It didn't help. I couldn't stop thinking about Mr. I-Want-To-Marry-Your-Mom. He was nothing like the guys she usually dated, and honestly, I didn't think my mom was the kind of lady he usually went out with, either. Could that be a good thing? I had no clue. That's why I was The Hook-up Doctor instead of Love Doctor.

But as much as I hated to admit it, even though he'd annoyed me, he almost seemed nice.

Still . . . I wasn't real sold on the whole happily-ever-after thing, and the thought of her getting all excited at the prospect, and then the drama when it all fell apart, left me feeling the need to kill as many zombies as possible.

Add that to the fact that Aspen and Pris bailed on us tonight. The night was completely blown to shit. Pretty much like the zombie heads I kept shooting off.

As soon as I got home from lunch, I'd texted Aspen. Like I said, she's the only one who knew how I felt about my mom, and it took her two hours to reply. Then she said she couldn't hang out tonight. I'm glad I didn't waste my time telling her what happened. If she didn't care enough to keep her plans with me, then I wasn't going to play Dr. Phil, spilling my guts to her like she could make it better or something.

"What's your problem tonight? You're looking a little angry there, Sebastian. Those zombies aren't really trying to take over the world." Jaden leaned against the video game. Around us, lights and bells went off. The arcade was packed like it was every weekend.

Game Over flashed across the screen.

"When are you going to realize you're not funny?" I asked him.

We started walking through the crowd. "Hey, I'm funny as hell. You're just mad because I get all the good lines in, and you're the sidekick."

This time I couldn't help but laugh. "Yeah, because we both know that's the truth." A couple of guys walked away from a table, and we sat down. "I'm mad and bored. We need to find something to do."

As if the seat shocked him, Jaden lurched forward. "Asketh and you shall receiveth. Behind you, six o'clock."

Slowly, I turned in my seat so I could look behind me without being too obvious. "What the?" Ice slithered through my veins. "What are the girls doing here?" Aspen and Pris sat in the back by the pool tables laughing and talking. They couldn't hang with us, but they could come here?

"Huh? Oh shit. I didn't even see them. Look to the left a little. Two blondes are looking this way."

I mentally scrolled through Aspen's text. "She said she didn't feel like hanging out tonight."

"Dude. Who cares? They ditched us. Get over it and check out—oh, she just waved. Let's go over there."

I was five feet ahead of Jaden, but I wasn't going

to the blondes. This weird heavy feeling weighed me down. Why wouldn't they want to chill with us? I'd needed to talk to her today, and she'd blown me off. As I stepped up to their table, Jaden grabbed my arm. "Wrong way, Romeo."

"They bailed on us." Why wasn't he upset about it?

"Like I said, who cares? Damn, Bastian. Maybe they wanted a chick night? There's no rule that we have to hang out with them every night. What's going on with you lately?"

Half of me knew he was right, but that didn't stop me from pulling my arm away from him, and plopping down at their table. "Fancy meeting you here." I crossed my arms so they knew I was mad. Pris's eyes got all wide, and Aspen stuttered when she talked.

"Hey! I, um . . . we were going to stay in, but changed our minds at the last minute."

That sounded awfully close to a line. Probably a line I'd given in the past, and it annoyed me that she not only used it with me, but that I let it bother me. "Whatever."

"Don't get your feelings hurt. It's not like you've never blown us off before," Pris said from across the table.

That wasn't the point, but if they didn't want to hang out with us, I didn't want to hang out with them, either. Two could play at that game. "I don't have my feelings hurt. Just thought I'd stop by and say hi. It actually worked out better for us anyway." I nodded my head toward the blondes who were looking our way. Both Pris and Aspen looked over. I pushed to my feet. "Have a good night, ladies."

When we walked away, Jaden grabbed my arm. "Hey, you sure you're okay?"

I peeked over my shoulder at Aspen and Pris, who were already off in some whispered conversation, then to the side at the blondes. My mind went to Roger and how he planned on officially moving in on my mom, like there was any point in taking relationships seriously. "Yep, I'm good. Come on, let's get ourselves some girls."

Hook-up Doctor,
I had my doubts, but I think it's actually working! I saw him this weekend and blew him off like you said. We were at the same get-together. He talked to me for a minute, and I played it off like it was no big deal. I swear, the whole night after that, he kept watching me. I'd look over, and he'd turn away, but I could tell he'd been looking at me. I kind of hate to admit it, but you actually

seem to know what you're talking about here. One question though . . . this is just a hypothetical. What would one do if it didn't work? If after one try, the guy didn't seem to notice you were ignoring him, should she try again? Again, just curious. You know, us inquiring minds and all. Thanks! Hope to hear from you soon.

  PA

CHAPTER FIVE

PA,

Huh, looks like ignoring people is in the air lately. At least for you, you have a good reason. Whatever. Not like I care. Glad everything's going as planned. Told you I was good. For now, you're going to want to just kick back. Give him some time to think. The more he thinks, the more confused he'll get, until he's thinking about you 24/7, which is what we want. In the meantime, play it cool. Maybe show up where he is, don't ignore him, but don't pay him too much attention, either. We like to be the center of attention, so if he feels you're kind of "eh" about him, guess who he'll start to want?

Hook-up Doctor

Two days passed, and I was still pissed. I'd never been ditched by a girl in my whole life. Now I had my so called BFF (and if I didn't stop using that word, I'd cut my own tongue out) was playing hooky on me like I was nothing. Was this how girls felt when I bailed on them? No. This was different. I always made sure girls knew up front I didn't do the dating thing. With Aspen, we were like yin and yang, soy burgers and tofu, Dawson and Joey . . . hell, I really needed to get a life.

I picked up my phone and scrolled through her texts. They started out with "I'm sorry" and by the hundredth one transformed into, "Whatever. It's not like you've never done it." So, apparently this whole thing was my fault. She was wrong, though. I never would have lied to her like that.

Glancing at the clock on my bedside table, I discovered I had a good two hours before my first shift at DJ's. I wasn't looking forward to it. On top of work, Mom and the loser, and the whole Pris/Aspen thing, I needed to do something to relax. Heading to my closet, I pulled out my guitar and leaned back on my bed again. My fingers moved across the strings with so much ease. It was almost like touching a girl; I knew just what to do, where to touch, and I enjoyed the hell out of it. My talent was the only thing I had that I could thank my mom's sperm donor, AKA my pops, for.

An hour later, I took a quick shower, put on the

black slacks and prep-school-looking green shirt and hoped like hell they wouldn't make me tuck it in. Jaden had some secret mission or something going on today so he was out as a possible ride to work. I knew he wasn't off with a girl, because he never kept his mouth shut about stuff like that. Jay had some kind of secrets going on that he didn't let the rest of us in on, but because of his sneakiness, getting to work was all up to me. Since I wasn't talking to the girls, once I had my shoes on, I grabbed my skateboard out of the closet.

I liked riding, but it was something I wanted to do for fun. Not to ride to my minimum wage job because I was too poor for a car and my friends had all decided to bail on me.

By the time I kicked my board up to walk into DJ's, I was sweating like crazy. Nice. And it was all Aspen and Pris's fault.

DJ showed me where to clock in and had Matt train me. I don't know what it was, but there was something about the guy that bugged me. He talked so much I had the urge to sock him in the face the whole time. You could tell he thought he knew everything and that rubbed me wrong.

Halfway through the shift, as he was teaching me how to make a meat supreme pizza, like it was so hard or something, and he nudged my arm. "So, is Aspen your girl?"

"Pfft, think again. I don't do the whole boyfriend/girlfriend thing," I said, while in my head I wondered why it was any of his damn business. Then a thought reared up inside me like an angry bull. Did this dude think he had a chance with her? I had a sort of sixth sense when it came to jerks. Maybe it had something to do with all the guys that came in and out of my mom's life, who knew.

What I did know was this wasn't the kind of guy I wanted Aspen with. He only wanted one thing from her. I could practically read his mind, because I thought the same things when it came to other girls. Which was totally different. "But I watch out for her. Make sure nobody hurts her and all that." Out of nowhere, something else tumbled out of my mouth. I didn't know where it came from and couldn't make it stop either. "Not that I have to do it real often. She doesn't date much. Her parents are real strict. They only let her date . . . hippies. Yeah, they have all sorts of rules. She's only allowed to go out with vegetarians who live in energy efficient houses."

And I was a friggin' idiot.

"No, shit?" Matt asked, one of his eyebrows rose like some cartoon character.

Luckily, he seemed to be an idiot, too. "Yeah, crazy, huh?" I tossed some pepperoni on the pizza. "They've been thinking about moving out to this hippie commune, so who knows, they might not be around much longer." My mind was screaming at me to shut the hell up, but I kept talking. "They make guys meditate with her dad before they let her leave with anyone. Something about being centered. I think it's some kind of hypnotizing thing, so they won't mess around with their daughter."

Apparently, I didn't know when to shut up. I'd been known to lay it on a little thick, I guess. Whatever. When he rolled his eyes, I knew I was losing him. "Dude, if you want her, all you had to do was say so."

Huh? What was he talking about? I didn't want Aspen. I was being a good friend. Taking care of her, so this guy didn't play around with her. The last thing I'd ever want was Aspen to get hurt. "You're barking up the wrong tree there, Mattie. I don't want Woodstock." I didn't.

Matt grabbed the pizza from in front of me and put it in the oven. "Matt. The name's Matt."

I ignored him. "So . . . do you? Want her, I mean?" My shoulders lifted in a shrug. "Just curious. Like I said, I take care of her."

Matt shook his head and laughed softly. I couldn't help but measure him up. You know, just in case I had to kick his ass. He was about my height, maybe an inch shorter, but I was definitely more muscular. I could take him no problem.

"I don't know. She's pretty cute. Funny, too. I saw her at the arcade a few days ago, but she was kind of being bitchy though."

He'd been there too? And what the hell? Who did he think he was calling her bitchy? "She's not a bitch."

"I didn't say she was. I said she was being bitchy. There's a difference."

Dude, what was wrong with me? I needed to get myself under control. "Don't take it personal, man." The tightness in my voice annoyed me. I don't know why I was still letting Friday night bother me so much. Made me feel a little better that he'd been there and she ignored him, too.

"Anyway, not sure. I'm pretty new in town so just getting the lay of the land, if you know what I mean." He put his hand in the air and I didn't leave him hanging even though his words rubbed me the wrong way. It was either give him five or punch him in the gut. Lay of the land? Who talked like that? *Me*.

"Sebastian! Matt! Back to work, guys. It's time for the dinner rush." DJ yelled at us.

The rest of the night, I took my anger out on pizza dough and tried not to think about Matt getting the lay of Aspen's land.

"Sebastian, get in the car."

I rode my skateboard down the street, ignoring Woodstock driving at my pace beside me.

"I swear, sometimes you're worse than a child. It's ten o'clock at night. I know your lazy butt doesn't want to walk home."

She was right. I didn't want to walk. I stank like pizza sauce, and all I wanted to do was get home and take a shower. "This doesn't mean I'm not mad at you."

"You're pouting," she teased after I got in.

"Only real men can pout without losing their masculinity. I have nothing to worry about there."

She laughed, and I couldn't help but laugh with her. That's why I avoided her. Even in the dark, all it took was knowing those green eyes were focused on me and I was a goner. My mom had the same power over me. I wondered how she couldn't know how much power she had. Mom, too. Why she let guys trample over her, when she had so much strength.

We took the ten minute drive in silence. A few

minutes later, she pulled into my driveway. Part of me didn't want to, but I couldn't help but talk to her. "Why'd you park here? I can walk."

Aspen hit the interior light and turned it on. "I figured I'd come in for a minute. I probably have some groveling to do, and I'd much rather do it inside than in my car." I knew she was trying to make me laugh, so I quirked up the left side of my mouth and gave her a half smile. Even though I wasn't over her ditching me yet, I was willing to talk about it. Like she always could, Aspen read between my lines and got out of the car. We were upstairs in my room a minute later. My mom wasn't home, but I still pushed the door closed, wanting privacy.

"Have you seen Pris or Jaden?" I asked after she sat down on my bed. I took the beat-up chair at my computer desk.

"Nothing from Jaden. Pris is at some fancy dinner thing with her family." Before I could reply, she sighed, and then started speaking again. "I'm sorry I lied to you. I just, I have my reasons, and I know I'm being shady, because I can't tell you why, but I would never have ditched you without a reason. There's just some stuff going on right now. Not like that makes it okay, because it was still wrong. You're my best friend, so that should always come first, but honestly,

I didn't think it would be that big a deal. I didn't know you'd be so mad."

I stared at her as she picked up my pillow and put it on her lap. One of her feet was tucked beneath her on my bed, while the other Nike-covered foot dangled near the floor. I couldn't stay mad at her even though I wanted to. "So, it's not just Jaden who says I'm your BFF. You think so, too." I crossed my arms and leaned back in the chair. It felt good to talk to her again. I couldn't handle not talking with Aspen, Pris, or Jaden.

"You know you are." She tossed the pillow at me. "Am I forgiven?" Aspen batted her eyelashes, and something flipped in my stomach.

"Whatever." I threw it back. "See, girls have it so easy. Smile and bat your eyelashes, and we're defenseless."

Aspen scooted my guitar over on the bed and leaned back further. "Whatever! Guys have it easy. Everything is much harder for girls."

"Pfft. Let's not go there. We'll just get in an argument again."

The room was quiet for a few minutes before she spoke. "So, is everything okay? It's not like you to get so upset about something like that." Her voice was all soft and caring, and I immediately felt like a wuss.

69

What was I supposed to say? Some dude who, if I'm honest with myself, looks like a nice guy wants to marry my mom, and I'm pissed about it? Oh, and on top of that, I'm confused about you right now. I didn't think so. There was no way those words were passing my lips.

"What do you mean, is everything okay with me? You're the one who said you have stuff going on right now. What is it, Woodstock? Do I need to beat someone up? Toilet paper a house? You name it, and I'm there."

"Smooth move on the subject change."

"Right back at ya."

Aspen sighed. "No, there's nothing you can do. It's—complicated. I love that you asked though." Her cheeks went a little pink, getting a smile out of me. I'd never seen her blush like that before.

"You know I always have your back." I scratched my head and realized I had pizza sauce in it. "I gotta get cleaned up real quick. I feel like a friggin' calzone. You should hang out though." I shrugged.

She glanced at her watch and I noticed her nails looked shiny like she had something on them. I'd never noticed that on her before. "Sure. I have time."

After pulling some clothes out of my drawers, I ran into my bathroom. I didn't stay in until I pruned like

I usually did, because I'd feel like a jerk making her wait. Five minutes later, a sauce-free Sebastian came out of the bathroom. I had on black, baggy basketball shorts that went down past my knees and no shirt.

"Um, are you going to put on any clothes?" Aspen had her shoes off as she leaned against my headboard. A little chill must have come in from my window, because shivers suddenly rolled down my spine.

"Why?"

Her cheeks went pink again.

Oh. *Ooh!* "You think I'm hot, too!" I practically shouted.

When her eyes bugged out, I realized I'd added the too on there. I couldn't think of a cover so I decided to embarrass her instead. "It's okay." I rubbed my stomach. "These abs have been known to bring down much tougher girls. I won't tell anyone you want me."

"You wish! I was thinking more along the line of your mom coming home and seeing you in your room alone with me, no shirt, and your boxer-briefs hanging out of your shorts."

My eyebrows raised and my heart started to beat faster. "You're taking your shirt off? Hell yeah."

Aspen launched herself off the bed and toward me. I easily caught her, and tackled her to the bed. My legs straddled her middle as I held her arms above her head. "I told you. I'm a ninja. Your tricks don't compare to my Jedi skills."

She tried to twist, but I held on to her. "Let me go."

"Not until you admit I kick ass." Actually, I just wanted to hold onto her a little longer. She was so soft beneath me. Smooth, female skin that drove me wild.

She bucked, her breathing coming out heavy, and that's when I realized what a huge mistake this was. This was A*spen*, and I was totally loving the feel of her. Totally savoring it. She smelled like cinnamon, and it was so much better than the floral stuff girls usually wore that it kind of hit me like a sock to the gut. It was suddenly all I could focus on. Her scent and feel. *What the hell*?! I jumped off her before she could realize I was enjoying it a little too much. This felt way different than BFF stuff.

First thing tomorrow, I was making some phone calls. I obviously needed some quality time of the female variety.

"You gave up." She sat up, smoothing her hair down and straightening out her baby blue t-shirt. It wasn't like a guy t-shirt, it was smaller, tighter, but definitely not revealing.

"No, I just felt bad beating you up after we just made up and all." I sat back in my chair, trying to get some distance between us. Maybe if I couldn't smell her, I could find a way to clear my head.

After a few silent minutes, she picked up my guitar that we thankfully hadn't kicked off my bed. "I haven't heard you play for a while."

"Yeah?" Playing for one person like that always felt like showboating.

"Play something before I go?"

No. "What do you wanna hear?"

She handed me the guitar, and I took it. "Something relaxing. I got tackled by this mental guy tonight, and it gave me a little headache." She smiled and gave me the eyes. Damn it with the girl eyes. I needed to figure out some kind of defense against it.

Aspen moved to the foot of my bed, crossing her legs beneath her. There was nothing I could do but sit back and play.

CHAPTER SIX

It had been a week since Aspen showed up at work to pick me up. For some reason, we'd only worked together once, but she still stopped by DJ's a lot. She and Pris would come flitting in for no apparent reason other than to taunt us with their freedom while we were knee deep in pizza dough. As quickly as they came in, they'd disappear again, leaving nothing behind but the urge to dump the uniform and go with them.

Matt talked me down from that a couple times. I think DJ wanted us to be pizza partners or something, because it seemed like every time I worked, Matt worked with me. Every time I worked with him, he bugged me more. I trusted him less.

"So, your first couple weeks on the job and you're already trying to get some time off, huh?" DJ asked me when I went into the back office to see about getting the weekend off for Pris's birthday. I did manage to weasel my way into an invite for me and Jaden. Of course, it hadn't been that hard. I guess they were kind of freaked out about staying the weekend by themselves anyway, but didn't want to tell her parents, because then they wouldn't be able to go.

We had it all figured out. I'd tell my mom I'd be spending the weekend with Jaden. Even though I never stayed at Jaden's I knew she wouldn't check up on me. It would be the perfect time for her to play house with the loser. Of course Pris and Aspen already had it figured out, because their parents totally trusted them and thought it was a good idea to rent a beach house for a couple teenage girls for the weekend. *Lucky*. And Jaden's parents just never gave a shit where he was. I'd be surprised if they even noticed he was gone.

Which sucked. My mom might be one of those girls who always thought she needed a man, but I knew she loved me. I wasn't sure Jaden could say the same thing when it came to his asshole parents.

Now, all I had to do was secure the time off, which I realized wasn't going to be so easy since I was not only new, but Aspen was taking the time off, too. "I'll make it up, DJ. Anytime you need me. It's Pris's birthday, and we've had this planned for months. I can't believe I spaced telling you about it when you hired me."

DJ sighed, and my stomach sank a little bit. I was

really looking forward to spending the weekend out of town with my friends. I figured it would be the best way for me to get back to normal . . . to hang out like we always did, and then the weirdness would be gone. Oh, and let's not forget beaches and bikinis, what guy wouldn't look forward to that?

"When is this happening again?"

"Next weekend. I can pick up extra shifts this week if you want me to. I'll be your go-to guy for the rest of the summer."

DJ kicked his feet up on his desk. "You have a knack for getting what you want, don't you?"

"Yep. I can show you how. Girls, favors, days off of work from cool ass bosses."

DJ laughed. "I'm married so no girls, and believe me, I'm not that cool."

I almost asked him why he tied himself down so young. He couldn't be any older than his mid-twenties, but I figured that wasn't the best way to get what I wanted. "Please?"

"Fine. Fill out the form, and you're good to go."

Hell yeah. "Thanks, man. I appreciate it. You need any other shifts covered, and I'm your guy."

"I'm holding you to that!" he called to me as I left the office.

The rest of my shift flew by. Mattie kept his mouth

shut, so I hadn't spent my whole shift annoyed. How could I be annoyed, anyway, since I would be getting a beach house for the weekend?

"Later guys!" I called out as I left.

On the way out, Matt stopped me. "Hey, there's a party tomorrow night."

"Where?" I asked, even though I was pretty sure I wasn't going. I liked to party, but didn't know about being all buddy-buddy with this guy.

"This girl I met at the mall. She said it's going to be a big one. Figured I'd let you know. She's pretty hot, and hot girls usually travel in packs."

I started to laugh, but then I remembered the guy annoyed me, so I didn't. "Yeah, maybe. I'll talk to my friends and see what's up." About that time Aspen, Pris and Jaden pulled in the parking lot to pick me up. Instead of Pris or Aspen's car, they were in the beatermobile. Weird.

Jaden rolled down the window. There was something sticking out of his lip.

"Dude! I told you I wanted to go with you. I want to get my lip done, too." Jerk. I couldn't believe he went without me. We'd done our eyebrows together and our lips were supposed to be next.

He smirked. "You couldn't handle it, Cinderella. Get in the car before your ride turns into a pumpkin."

"Catch ya later," I said to Matt as I walked off. Unfortunately, he was following me. Well, not me, I guess, because he was walking to the back door where Aspen sat with her window open.

"You're still going tomorrow night, right?" he asked her. My footsteps stilled. Looked like me and Mattie here needed to have a talk. Wasn't he just talking about girls at the party, and now he'd invited Aspen, too? That so wasn't going to fly.

"Yep," she replied to him, running a hand through her honeyed hair. My hand started to twitch. When she leaned toward the front and started talking to Pris, I let the air out of my lungs. She was hardly giving him the time of day, like she didn't really care that he was there, which was cool. It would be a lot easier to break it to her that I thought the guy was a chump.

I slipped around him and leaned toward the window. "Hey, Woodstock." I picked a piece of paper out of her hair and man, I wanted to do it again. It was just as soft as it looked. The urge hit me to turn around and tell him, "See, I can touch her whenever I want to," but then I realized that was a little bit creepy. Like I wanted her or something, and really, I just wanted to keep her away from guys like him and . . . well, me.

"Um, hey, Bastian."

I opened the door. Aspen scooted over, and I slid in beside her. "Count me and Jaden in tomorrow night too, could you, Mattie?" As if Jaden could read my mind, he laughed, then peeled out of the parking lot.

PA,

Time to step up your game. It's time for Operation Flirt. Now, I know I don't know you, but just from your emails, you don't seem like a real flirty type. Unlike what some girls think, flirting is an art form. It's not something everyone can do. I think you can handle it, though, and it goes a long way when it comes to getting the guy.

There's a fine line between being flirty and looking easy. You don't want to look easy because, despite what we try and make girls think, we really don't want an easy girl, just like I'm sure girls don't want an easy guy. Let me know if you have any questions.

Hook-up Doctor

Hook-up Doctor,

Okay, I feel like an idiot that I'm asking your advice on how to flirt, but I since I already look desperate enough by doing this, I figured what the heck. Helps that you don't know who I am, too, but we'll just pretend it's because I really don't care what people think. LOL.

This is the thing, I've flirted a bit. I mean, what girl hasn't, but it's hard to know what guys really want. It's not like we can ask, and since I'm paying you, I guess I should fully take advantage of the situation, right?

There are those girls who walk around half-naked, plastering themselves to guys and for some strange reason, guys seem to go for that. Isn't that an easy girl? You said guys don't want easy, then what do they want? I have to be honest with you, the whole half naked thing is not me, and though I really want this guy, I'm not comfortable turning into someone I'm not for him. Is that what you're asking for? Be honest, is that really what guys want in a girl? I have a party coming up, and I'm thinking it will be a good opportunity to put my flirting into action.

Thanks,
PA

PA,

While the half-naked thing is good on the eyes, it's really not what we want (shh, don't tell though). We want confident, but not bitchy. You want to be sexy and fun, but still in control, know what I mean? You don't have to try and control us, but if we're turned on, it will happen regardless. Control is everything. It not only makes you more desirable (strong women are hot), but it's also better for you. You know, safety and all, especially if there's a party. Don't give up that control, PA. You can do this. Let me know how it goes.

Hook-up Doctor

Jaden stood in front of the mirror in my room, ruffling his hair so it looked extra messy. He cracked me up. Sometimes he was worse than a girl with his primping. "How ya doin' over there, Goldilocks? Do you need me to give you a perm before we go? Oh, and I think your roots are showing. Might be time to pull out the peroxide again."

He looked at me in the reflection. "It takes time to look this hot. Maybe I should give you some lessons."

"I don't need to try. I'm always hot."

Jaden shook his head at me. Ha. No comeback for that one.

"So, what's up with this party tonight?" he asked.

I pulled on my black button up shirt, leaving it open so you could see my Beastie Boys t-shirt under it. I didn't care how old school they were. People either gave me shit about them or looked at me confused because they didn't know who they were. Not my fault they didn't know good music. Plus, it was my lucky shirt. Tonight, I needed some luck.

After buckling my belt so that my shorts didn't fall off, but still sat low like I liked them, I walked to the other mirror to put in the new barbell my mom got me for my eyebrow. "Who knows? Figured it would be better than chillin' at home. According to Mattie, there's supposed to be no shortage of hot girls there."

Once he had his hair effectively messed up, Jaden sat in my computer chair and pulled on his shoes. "Nice. Hopefully, there will be some fresh meat."

Which was exactly what I needed. My head had been all screwed up lately. I wasn't sure what was going on. "That's what he said. Idiot."

Jaden laughed. "You don't like him?"

I shrugged. "I don't know. I don't trust him. He

was asking about the girls." Only a slight lie. He'd asked about one of the girls, but Jaden didn't need to know that. He'd only take it to mean the wrong thing, and I didn't feel like getting into it tonight.

Jaden played with his new piercing before he said, "Speaking of, Pris has been acting weird lately. I'm wondering if all her parents' money is making her crazy. It's like she's had split personalities or something. One minute she's fine, and then she seems extra pissed at me for some reason."

Feeling my pockets, I made sure I had my cell and wallet and then headed out the door. Jaden was right behind me. "She's a girl. They're always weird. And no offense, bro, but she's always a little pissy with you."

"True. What's up with that?"

I shrugged, because really, I had no clue. All I wanted to focus on tonight was having a good time. I felt pumped, my pulse break-dancing beneath the surface of my skin. I needed a night out to get my head straight. It was strange—the way I felt so off my game lately. I wasn't sure what was going on, but I planned on rectifying it tonight. "You sure we shouldn't take the beatermobile? You know, just in case. That way we don't have to depend on the girls?" I asked Jaden, halfway hoping he'd say yes while the other half wanted him to say no.

His eyes diverted away from mine. "It's not really runnin' too well. Might be smarter just to ride with them."

I didn't know why Jaden was embarrassed about his car. I gave him crap about it, but he was right, at least he had one. "K. We'll look at it on my next day off. See if we can figure out what's up." I would, too. Even though I didn't do the whole car-work thing, I would help Jaden if push came to shove. I tried to pull the door open, but he stopped me.

"Yeah, right. We all know you don't like to get dirty." He laughed, but then turned serious. "Can I stay here tonight though? My dad's being a prick."

I had a feeling there was a lot more going on at Jaden's than he let on, but I didn't dare ask him. It was some kind of guy code or something. He knew I was there for him, and if he wanted to talk to me, he would, just like if I ever felt like spilling my guts about my mom, I knew Jaden would listen. It wasn't something we did, and I knew it would only embarrass him if I brought it up. "Yeah. Anytime. Stay as long as you want. I was going to ask, but I forgot." It would make him feel better if he thought it was my idea. I threw my arm over his shoulder. "Come on, man. We're going to make sure this night is epic."

"That's what I'm talking about." Then we were out the door to Aspen's house. No matter what it took, I was going to make sure this was a night we didn't forget.

CHAPTER SEVEN

The living room was crowded with bodies almost as tightly as the sea of people at the Green Day concert I went to the year before. I pushed my way through the crowd, Aspen holding on to my shirt from behind, Pris holding her, and Jaden bringing up the rear. My stomach was a little uneasy for some reason, so I wanted to find a quiet place for our little pow-wow. The kitchen was much less crowded than the living room, but still not quite what I was looking for, so I slipped out the back door and waited for them to join me.

"Um, party's inside, bro," Jaden said.

"I know, I just wanted to figure out the night." I looked at my cell phone. "It's 9:30 now so we have to be out of here in three hours to make curfew. We still doing the three drink max for the rest of us and Pris is the designated driver?"

They all nodded "Bet. Text if you need us, k?" I said to Pris and Aspen. I knew how guys thought—especially when there was alcohol involved. I knew what was always on my mind, so Jaden and I were always sure we kept an eye on the girls when we were out. There was this one time a guy got a little too touchy feely with Pris, but luckily she'd been smart enough to give him a right hook and find Jaden and me. After that we always came up with a pre-party plan, also known as the PPP just to be on the safe side. "Don't do anything I would do." I smiled at the girls, my eyes lingering a little longer on Aspen. My stomach flipped.

"You're so funny, Bastian. It's okay for *you* to mess around, but not us." Aspen put her hands on her hips like she was annoyed. She wore something different tonight. Maybe something of Pris's because I'd never seen her wear it before. It didn't show a lot of skin like the stuff I'd admired on the other girls as we walked through the house, but it was definitely more when it came to Aspen. It was a red—which I'd always thought looked hot on a girl—sleeveless V-neck that teased, but didn't really show the goods. A little teardrop-looking necklace hung down and rested between her breasts. And she topped off the outfit with a pair of hip hugging jeans that almost made me groan.

Yeah, I definitely needed to be here to watch the girls tonight.

Luckily, I was pretty good at playing things off when

I wanted to, so instead of admiring her, I nudged her. "Hey, you know I'm all for equal flirting rights and all that, but I also gotta take care of my girls." Damn, I was a pretty nice guy when I thought about it.

"If we don't see each other before, let's meet up at 11:00," I said. If we came together, we left together, so we liked to meet up to make sure everyone was still having a good time. All for one and shit. I pushed my hands in my pockets, feeling pretty proud of myself. We got the pre-party plan out of the way and now it was time for the night of epicness to begin.

"Alright, *Dad*. See you guys later." Aspen started to pull Pris away, and when she did, I saw Pris lean over and whisper something to her. Aspen shook her head no, while turning back to look at us. Pris nodded, Aspen smiled and they disappeared into the kitchen.

"They're being weird," I told Jaden.

"Who?" he asked, his eyes already scanning the kitchen through the glass door.

He had the right idea, so I mumbled a "Nothing." After straightening my shirt, I looked over at Jaden. "Are you ready for our night of epic proportions?"

He gave his hair another ruffle with his hand to make sure it was effectively messy. "I was born ready."

Blood pumped through my veins with so much fervor, I didn't even take the time to tell Jaden how corny his last line was. I strode into the kitchen with my boy at my side, on a mission. We were going to find girls, and I was going to get my head on straight, because no good could come from the urge I'd fought to pull Aspen back to me as she'd been swallowed by the crowd.

Mattie hadn't been wrong about the ratio of female vs. males. There was a good two to one, which were odds I really liked. In fact, there were so many girls dancing around that I was having a hard time choosing which one I wanted to go for.

"Dude, you've found something wrong with every girl. I'm about to play this one solo if you can't make up your mind." Jaden leaned against the wall next to me. A fireplace with a mantle full of pictures of who I assumed was Mattie's Mall Girl was behind him.

"We're not trying to decide between a Big Mac or a chicken sandwich here. This is some serious shit. We want epicness, we have to be choosy."

Jaden rolled his eyes, so I continued to scan the room.

"What about them?" he asked, pointing to a red head and girl with dark brown hair who were dancing with each other. My body perked up at the sight. "I'll take Red and you can have the other one," he said.

"Nah, I'm not feelin' her." I was starting to get a little worried about myself. I mean, this was a party, and there were chicks everywhere, but none of them were really getting my blood pumping, if you know what I mean. What guy wasn't trying to hook-up at this party?

Apparently, me . . .

"Okay, Sebastian. You pick, but I'm telling you, if you don't pick some girls within five minutes, I'm out. I at least want to get some dancing in, rather than staring at your frown all night." Jaden pushed off the wall and crossed his arms over his chest.

"I'm frowning?" Why was I frowning?

"Yeah, you've looked pissy ever since we left the girls. I think you've been hanging out with them too long. You're swapping testosterone for estrogen. I feel like you're going to start lecturing me on seeing women as more than a piece of meat any minute." I opened my mouth, but Jaden cut me off. "Which I do. You know that, but I also want to have a good time, and if there's a girl I meet who I like and we're both willing, there's nothing wrong with that."

I groaned. He was right.

About that time a set of twins, *freaking twins* walked up to us. They had black hair, blue eyes and curvy little bodies that I suddenly really, really wanted to get to know better. "Wow, how did we miss you ladies all night?" I took a step closer, eagerness making my pulse rock out.

"I was wondering the same thing," Jaden said from beside me.

"I'm Abby," the taller one who stood across from Jaden said. "And this is my sister, Crystal."

"Do you want to dance?" I asked in my most suave voice. Yeah, I knew it was lame, this whole game guys and girls played, but what could I do about it? People had been doing it way before The Hook-up Doctor was around, and they'd do it long after as well.

"I'd love to," she replied. I looked over to see Jaden and whatever her name was already locked in an embrace. I slid my hands to her waist as she wrapped hers around my neck. The song was fast, but we didn't care. Her body slinked against mine, and for a minute, all I could think was, "hell yes", but then I remembered I hadn't checked my phone for a while. What if Aspen or Pris had texted, and I didn't hear it?

Let me tell you, it's not easy to slip your cell phone out of your pocket all incognito with a girl slinking her body as close to you as she can. Somehow, I managed it. While she was distracted, rubbing her hand through my hair, which annoyed the crap out of me, I checked my phone for messages behind her back.

Nothing.

Instead of being all mopey like I had for most of the night, I tried to get into what I was doing. I had a pretty girl in my arms. A guy definitely shouldn't have to talk himself into enjoying that. "Do you live around here?" I asked close to her ear, inhaling a deep breath. Damn. *Flowers.* I hated that crap.

"No. My sister and I are staying with my cousin for the summer. It's her house."

"That sucks. I'd love to get out of this place for the summer, and you're stuck here."

Her hand traveled up my back. "I don't know . . . I think I'm starting to enjoy it."

Ding! Ding! Ding! Every warning bell in my body erupted. I was pretty sure she just told me I'm the reason she was starting to enjoy herself. "Me—" too I tried to say, but just about that time, Aspen caught my eye on the other side of the room. She stood with some guy, her arms flailing around as she spoke animatedly. She cracked me up when she got excited like that, talking with her body just as much as she did her mouth. I chuckled.

The guy pulled her close to him, and they started to sway to the music just like I was doing with Crystal, but all of a sudden, I wasn't laughing any more. The muscles in my body tightened, like I'd worked them out too hard and got a cramp. I was sweating and felt like I'd had too much to drink when I hadn't.

"You what?"

"Huh?" I asked, startled. I couldn't believe I almost forgot I was dancing with this girl.

"You said 'me', but then you stopped."

Get it together, Bastian. What's wrong with you?

"Nothing. I guess I'm pretty lucky you decided to come for a visit, huh?"

I could hear the smile in her voice when she replied, "Maybe."

I tried to focus on the girl in my arms, I really did, but my eyes kept darting to the other side of the room. The guy dancing with Aspen tried to slide his hand under the back of her shirt, and I stiffened, immediately pulling away from Crystal. Aspen did the same with hand boy over there, turning her nose up at him in a playful way and walking away. *That's my girl.*

"Are you okay?" Crystal stepped back and looked at me. The girl was beautiful. There was no reason in the world I should be so distracted, but I was.

"Want to just chill for a minute?" As much as I wanted to be into her, I wasn't right now, and I didn't want to lead her on.

She bit her bottom lip and then smiled. I found the quietest corner of the room that I could, but one that still gave me vision to scope out the living room in case I was needed. I stood in the corner, with Crystal in front of me. She showed a lot of skin. Way more than Aspen, but not quite as much as Alex did, which was nice. "So, I think it must have been your cousin who met this guy I work with. He's the one who told me about the party."

Crystal ran her hands down her shirt as if she was trying to smooth it out. "Matt or something like that? Paula told me about him."

"They hooking up?" I asked, not sure why I cared. Okay, so that's a lie, if they were hooking up, I knew he couldn't have Aspen because she wouldn't be down for that. Which meant she couldn't get hurt, and I could go back to being my normal self.

"I don't think so. They didn't, yet at least. Who knows what will happen tonight though."

Great. There went that plan.

We talked for a little while. She was pretty cool, liked to laugh, and I found out her boyfriend dumped her when she told him she was leaving for the summer. "That sucks. Sounds like a jerk, but it's probably better, anyway." It was pretty obvious I wasn't going to hook-up with this girl tonight, and I was okay

94

with that. I wasn't feelin' this whole thing, and she seemed to still be caught up on her ex. My night of epicness was turning out to be anything but. She was pretty fun to talk to though, so I didn't mind.

"Why?" she asked.

"What's the point? Relationships never last anyway. Better to end them quick rather than drag things out." I didn't care how jaded I sounded, it was how I felt. Anyone who had seen what I had would feel the same.

"A guy who doesn't believe in love? Wow, I don't run across that every day." We'd never see eye to eye on this, so I just shrugged, scanning the room for my friends. I saw Pris standing alone in a corner, her mouth tight. She obviously wasn't having a good time. Just as I was about to tell Crystal I needed to go check on my friend, I saw Aspen with another dude. He had this cocky smirk on his face and she was looking up at him batting her eyelashes in a way I'd never seen her do before.

What was she doing? She put an arm around the guy's shoulders and he did the same to her. They were laughing. With each passing second that they stood there, him looking at her like she was his perfect score for the night, my gut started to squeeze tighter. Was she flirting with this guy? And if she was, which was super freakin' weird because I'd never seen Aspen flirt before, why couldn't I take my eyes off her?

"Aw, so she's the reason you've been distracted all night?"

I glanced at Crystal, back over at Aspen and then at Crystal again. "I haven't been distracted." *Yeah right.*

"It's okay." She sighed. "I think I was using you to get my mind off Will, so we're even."

This time, my vision jerked toward her. "What? I'm not into her. She's my B—" I groaned. Why did I keep saying BFF? I swear, it was like Paris Hilton took me over. "She's my friend. I watch out for her. That's all."

In the sea of people, I found Aspen again. She stood up on her tip-toes and whispered in the guy's ear. "Dude, what's she doing?"

I didn't realize I'd spoken out loud until Crystal answered me. "Flirting." Aspen stumbled. "She looks a little drunk."

"Nah, we have a three drink rule in the PPP."
"PPP?"

"Pre-party plan. She doesn't drink much anyway. I don't think she's ever gone past one drink." A memory popped into my head. "Oh! There was this one time Pris's parents were out of town. I dared her to drink this fierce drink Jaden made, and she was gone. Stumbling all over the place like—" Holy hell. Like she was doing now. "I gotta go."

Crystal grabbed my arm as I tried to walk away. "I guess I was wrong, you do believe in love."

"Pfft." I tried not to roll my eyes. I didn't do love, and if I did, it wouldn't be with my best friend. "It's not that. She's just a friend." My mouth felt all sticky. As I looked over, a hand grabbed onto Aspen's arm and started leading her down the hall. *Not going to happen, dumbass*. I pushed my way through the crowd, grabbing him right before they made it to a door. "Thanks, bro. I got her from here."

His eyes narrowed at me. "Who the hell are you?"

I ignored him. "Come on, Woodstock. Let's get you out of here." Standing this close to her, I could see she was definitely trashed. Her big, green eyes were droopy, with pink tinting the white part.

"I'm okay, Baaaasssstian. Tad's just helping me find a bathroom." She patted his chest.

"Well, now I am. You can go," I told him. About then, Aspen grabbed her stomach. "Oh, crap. I think I'm going to get sick." She swayed a little. About that time, Tad took off, and I pushed the door open. Bathroom my ass, it was a bedroom with a big empty bed. I'd have to remember his face so I could kick his ass next time I saw him.

"Uggg." Aspen groaned.

"We'll get you to the bathroom." She stumbled, so I picked her up, pushing doors open until I found the bathroom. When she was on her feet, I locked the door behind us, and that's when it happened. Instead of aiming for the toilet, Aspen faced me. Green puke flew all over my not-so-lucky-anymore shirt. *Ugh!* She freaking owed me for this. I turned her toward the toilet, and let her finish. With her hair in my hands, she emptied her stomach. I kept feeling it threaten to bubble up in my throat, but I held it down. Puke and I didn't go well together. The last thing we needed was one of us up-chucking in the toilet while the other took the bathtub.

When she finally finished, I helped her to her knees, rubbing her back. *Please don't puke. Please don't puke.* What was it with girls and alcohol? Boys always get the bad name, but I'd never drunk so much I blew chunks. "It's okay," I told her when she started to cry.

"I hate being sick," Aspen mumbled. I kept smoothing her hair down and sliding my hand over her back.

"You okay?"

"No . . ." her eyes were starting to close, but she kept popping them open again.

"I'm here, Woodstock. Are you going to be sick again?"

She shook her head. I grabbed some tissue, wet it and wiped her face. I felt like an idiot, but I knew she wouldn't want to go out there like this. I pulled off both my shirts, and tossed my puke covered, Beastie Boys shirt in the trash, before putting the other one back on. I wanted to cry myself. That was a nice shirt. "I'm going to pick you up." She mumbled something which I assumed was an okay. Bending down, I pulled her into my arms. "Let's get you home." Her reply was to wrap her arms around my neck.

Everywhere that she touched me, it was like little currents of electricity sparked beneath my skin. It was weird as hell, but kind of felt good, too. As soon as I hit the front door, both Jaden and Pris were by my side.

"What happened?" Pris asked. At the same time, Jaden said, "Is she okay?"

"We're good. Just a little too much to drink."

When we got to the car, Jaden somehow made sure Aspen was strapped in, while she was still lying down with her head in my lap.

"I don't know how I'm going to get her into my house like that, Bastian. My parents will freak," Pris said from the front seat.

I pushed her soft hair away from her face. "She can come home with me. I'm pretty sure my mom's out."

Pris dropped us all off at my place. Jaden stayed downstairs, planning to sleep on the couch, and I carried Aspen up to my room. After I had her all tucked in, I started to walk away.

"Bastian . . . Don't go." Her voice was hardly over a whisper.

I closed my door and locked it. "I'm right here."

A smile curved her lips, and then she was out. There was nothing I could do but fall into my torn-up computer chair and wonder how I got myself into this mess. The goal for the night had been freedom. To find a girl who was interested, listen to music, dance and get my mind off of all this other heavy stuff: to forget mom and the loser, to forget my Aspen confusion, to help Jaden block out whatever was going on at home. Instead, I ended up with green vomit on my not-so-lucky shirt and sitting in my cramped chair, while I watched a girl sleep in my bed.

Here was my epicness, because despite how things turned out, I wouldn't be anywhere else. I wouldn't want anyone else to take care of her. To watch her sleep. To hold her hair. To carry her to the car. Of course, I could have done without the puke part for both of our sakes, but besides that, I'd rather be with her than anyone else. I'd rather be here than dancing with Crystal or any other girl.

That's when it hit me. How had I been so dumb? How could I be such an idiot? And when the hell did it happen? When had things changed or had they always been like this, but I didn't realize it?

Looked like I did do love, and I was in it with my best friend.

I was so fucked.

CHAPTER EIGHT

Now, I'm not a scientist or anything, but I figured every theory needed to be tested. And so far, that's what the whole think-I'm-in-love-with-my-best-friend thing was—a theory. I mean, I'd never been in love before. How did I know for sure? It could have been lack of female attention, rebellion, or, I don't know, delirium or something. Stranger things had happened. Jumping to the conclusion it was love, was just a . . . what's it called? Hypothesis? My science teacher would be so proud. The way I saw it, I wasn't educated enough in love to make an educated guess about it. Especially since I wasn't even sure I believed in it.

I wasn't sure I'd ever really seen anyone in love before. My dad obviously didn't love my mom, since he bailed on us. He obviously hadn't loved me, either. Mom thought she was in love a lot, but look how all those relationships turned out. Either people put too much stock in something that was so easy to fall in and out of, or love and my family just didn't jive.

Before I pledged my undying devotion (not that I'd ever do that), but before I decided if I wanted to do anything about this or not, I needed to figure it out.

The thing was, I wasn't sure how to do that. Would ignoring her, showing up where she was or flirting with her do the trick like it did with my clients? I could always try making out with her, which I'd enjoy a whole lot, but:

1. I was pretty sure if I started kissing Aspen out of the blue, I'd be talking with a high pitched voice when she finished with me.
2. Love wasn't supposed to only be about kissing, right? I mean, I did that with the other girls, and I knew damn well I didn't love them.

The Hook-up Doctor was in uncharted territory, and it sucked.

I clicked the red square in the right corner of my inbox. PA hadn't replied back to me, so I didn't know how her attempted flirt-fest had gone. Hopefully, it worked out for her. At least somebody should get what they wanted, even if it wasn't me. Of course, that could be because I had no idea what that was, but why keep score?

When I turned to walk toward my closet to get my

guitar, a soft rapping came from my bedroom door. I groaned knowing it would be my mom. I *so* wasn't in the mood for her shiny-happy-people impersonation today. I made a quick U-turn anyway and opened the door. "Hey, Ma."

"Hey, kiddo. Do you work today?" She walked into my room and stole my chair. I plopped down on my bed, figuring we must be due for some big, important conversation that I had no interest in having. She never came into my room, so this had to be big. Fear trickled through me, gaining speed. Had Roger asked her? Was she getting married? Had he broken up with her? Hurt her? I bit all that back and answered her question instead.

"In a couple hours. What's up?" I tried to focus on my bed and how it still smelled like Aspen's cinnamon. I took a big whiff and at the same time, realized I'd totally freakin' lost my mind. I was trying to sniff my bed? If this was love, it really screwed with you.

"Are you still going to be with Jaden this weekend?" She looked nervous, picking at something on her skirt. Uh-oh. Here we go. The fear gained strength.

"Yeah."

"Roger asked me to go away with him for the weekend. We're thinking a little bed and breakfast by the coast and—"

I held up my hand. "Really don't want the details, Ma." Especially when I could think of my own. Not the do-not-disturb kind because that made me want to vomit in my mouth, but if old Rog wanted to propose, a weekend at a little bed and breakfast at the coast would be the perfect time for him to do it. Jerk. What was the point in asking me if he didn't plan to wait for my reply?

I couldn't say any of that though. Not only did she not know I knew, but I could see the sparkles in her eyes, and the last thing I wanted to do was be the one to dim them. So I shrugged. "Sure. Whatever. I won't be here anyway." It didn't even strike me as weird that Mom was pretty much asking my permission to go away with a guy. She did a lot of stuff I didn't agree with, but we'd always been a team. Whenever some chump broke her heart, I was the one who helped her put it back together again. That's just how we worked.

A smile stretched across her face. "He's special, Sebastian. Really, Roger is different."

My eyes automatically started to roll, but I stopped them when a picture of Woodstock slipped into my head. I tried to push it out, but it kept playing over and over. Glue stuck my mouth together, and it was like part of me wanted to pry it open, but the other part wanted to clamp it shut. How lame would it be to ask my mom about girls? Hell, I knew more about women than guys like Roger who were twice my age. But this wasn't just a girl, it was *Aspen*. She was different.

I peeked around my room, half-expecting to see a hidden camera or Jaden camped out in the corner to catch me slipping. When I was sure we were alone, I scratched an invisible itch on my head so my arms blocked my vision of Mom sitting across from me. "So, how do you, um . . . know you love him or whatever?"

I felt like such a loser. I was The Hook-up Doctor. I was supposed to know girls. Know *myself*, and here I was, asking my mom how she knew when she was in love. When did my life become such an epic fail? When did I lose control of everything?

When she didn't reply, I dropped my arm to look at her. Silver-dollar sized eyes met my stare. I'd totally just screwed up. She'd never let me live this down, and unlike with Jaden, she wouldn't be teasing me, she'd be hopeful. That was much worse. "Not for me! I'm too young and having too much fun to go and think I'm in love, it's just . . . Jaden—yeah, Jay met this girl and he's all whipped over her and asking me how he knew if he loved her or not, so I figured it couldn't hurt to ask." And ramble. Since when did I start rambling? First to Mattie about Aspen and the hippie stuff and now this.

I could practically see the happy sigh fall from my mom's mouth. I'm sure her heart was doing some love dance pitter-patter in her chest. "It's okay, you know, Sebastian. My mistakes and your dad's, that doesn't—"

"Ma!" I interrupted her. "Not going there, okay? I said it wasn't about me. Let's not play Oprah." I stood up and grabbed my shoes. What the hell had I been thinking?

She stopped me with her words. "Okay then, tell Jaden that I can't really explain it. It's just something you know. You want to take care of them and let them take care of you, too. They make you happy like no one else can."

I tossed my shoes to the floor and sat back down. This was a huge mistake. Like making out in Alex's room sized mistake, but I couldn't stop myself from asking anyway. "But is it worth it? All the times you've been hurt? How do I, I mean how does Jaden know that he won't get left or end up hurting her?" I'd seen my mom cry so many tears, some of them shed because of my own dad, that I wasn't sure I could risk doing that to Aspen.

"Oh, honey." Mom got up and sat next to me on my bed. My legs itched to get up and blow off this whole conversation, but they were too heavy. Like something weighed them to the ugly brown carpet of my bedroom. "You never know what's going to happen. You have to have faith. All the heartache I've felt *is* worth it. I've met Roger, and I'm willing to risk heartache because, not only do I think he's worth it, but I'm worth it."

I couldn't really understand what she meant. Sure, it's easy to say something was worth it, but I didn't know if I agreed. How did you know beforehand if it really was worth it? How did you know if you could deal with the aftershocks? I didn't know if I wanted to risk it. What if I was right and the whole love thing was just a crock, and I ended up losing Aspen? My best friend?

"I think Jaden should go for it. For the first time in a long time, my life feels pretty much perfect. I have the world's best son and a boyfriend that I love. There's nothing else I want."

I huffed, trying to sound lighter than I felt. "You're such a girl."

Mom hugged me. "I love you, Sebastian, and you tell Jaden I don't think he has to ever worry about hurting a girl. He may not want to admit it, but his heart is always in the right place."

We both knew we weren't talking about Jaden. "Hmm, maybe he can use that excuse in the future when he's being an idiot."

She laughed. "Probably not a good idea." Then she sighed and added, "You're the best thing in my life, Sebastian. I'm so lucky to have you."

This was getting way too heavy for me, so I quirked my brow at her, still as confused as ever. "Yeah, that's what all the girls say, Ma."

Aspen picked me up since we both worked the same shift that night. It was weird, the erratic thump of my pulse, like I was nervous to be around her or something. Sebastian Hawkins didn't get nervous around girls. It made me feel like a fish out of water. No, that was kind of a lame analogy. A fish out of water probably felt as though it was dying, and I didn't feel that. My palms were sweaty, my heart beating like a drum, my muscles all twitchy as if I was jacked up on five triple shots of espresso.

"Hey, you okay over there?" she touched my leg with those new, shiny nails I was still unused to. I looked over at her, in her matching DJ's polo shirt and smiled. Well, I tried to smile, but it felt more like a grimace. "You're being weird, and you look like you're going to puke." She swatted me. "Oh my God, Sebastian, are you *on* something?"

Yeah, the crazy train, because I think I might be in love with you. "Hell no. You know I paid attention to all those, 'this is your brain. This is your brain on drugs,' lessons in health. I don't mess with that shit."

She shrugged. "I know, but, I don't know. Things have been different lately. I just wanted to be sure you're still the same old Sebastian I know and love."

I love you, too. What the hell was wrong with me? Someone needed to shoot me before I could fully morph into some slobbering lovesick puppy. "Nah, I'm the same. You're the same. Nothing's changed." Except nothing was the same. Everything was different.

Aspen laughed, and little tremors went off inside me. Her laugh made me want to do it, too. She was quiet for a minute before she sighed. "It's inevitable, you know. Things change."

"Not us." I didn't want to lose her. That was my biggest fear. So many people came in and out of my life. Besides my mom, Jaden, Pris, and Aspen had been the only ones who stayed. "You'll always be my little hippie, Woodstock." My fingers itched to reach out and grab her. To do the hand holding thing I swore I would never do.

A smile tilted her lips. "Except, I'm not a hippie. You know that."

She was right. She'd never been quite as bad as her parents. When I realized she didn't argue with the part where I said she was mine, I fell back into the seat, and relaxed for the first time since getting in the car. "I know. You're just you. That's what makes you so damn cool. I mean, Sebastian Hawkins isn't best friends with just anyone." And she was one of the cool girls. The one I told PA most guys don't notice. I hadn't. Not until recently at least.

Aspen laughed again. "No one makes me laugh like you. Things have been kind of screwy with me lately. I still feel bad about bailing on you. Want to hang out after work tonight? Unless you're going out or something."

My stomach got all heavy. This was the perfect chance to test my hypotheses. For the first time in my life I was excited about a science experiment. "For you, Woodstock, my schedule is completely open." Now, I only had to hope once I had my answer, I'd know what to do about it.

"I'm going to run home and get cleaned up, and I'll be back over," I told Aspen when we pulled into her driveway at about 11:30 that night.

"Can you use my window? I don't want my parents to know you're over so late."

I groaned. "Just sneak me in. All the lights are already off, so you know they're in bed." Yeah, I know I was being lazy, but the whole window thing was lame. Plus, heights were kind of scary.

Even in the blackness of the night, I could still see the Aspen scowl on her face. I faltered for a minute, almost telling her I'd climb the stupid side of her house, but I was tired after a long day of making pizza so, instead, I just said, "Please?"

She stomped her foot. "Fine. You're so spoiled, Bastian. I'll be at my door in fifteen minutes. If you're not there, you're not coming in." She stormed away before I could reply. With an extra bounce in my step (yes, I'm fully aware at how stupid that sounds), I ran to my house and let myself in. I took another speed shower, got dressed and then knocked lightly on my mom's bedroom door. The light shined from under her door, so I knew she was awake. Probably reading one of those puke-worthy romance books she liked.

"Come in," she called out. I pushed the door open enough just to stick my head inside. Sure enough she was curled up in her bed with a book that had a guy on the cover with longer hair than her.

"I'm going to go over to Aspen's to watch a movie. I'll be back late." Mom was pretty lenient, but more so when it came to Aspen. I had a curfew just like the next guy, and if I told her I was going to any other girl's house to watch a movie at midnight I'd get a big hell no. But because it was Woodstock, I got a smile.

"Have fun. Tell her I said hi."

"Thanks, Ma." I jogged over to the bed, gave her a hug and then bailed. I knew Aspen well enough to know if I wasn't at her door when she got there, she wouldn't give me another chance. I liked that about her.

As soon as I stepped up to the porch, the door slid open slowly. I took off my shoes and left them on the porch, sneaking upstairs in my socks. The cool thing was, her parents had done some remodeling a few years back and their room was downstairs on the other end of the house. We were pretty safe up here, as long as we were quiet.

"What do you want to watch?" she asked. For the first time since I got inside, I really looked at her. She'd taken a shower, too, because her hair was wet, tied in some kind of bun thing on top of her head. Her contacts were out and a pair of wire-rimmed glasses sat on her nose. She wore a pair of black pajama pants with a purple tank-top.

And, holy shit, did I want to touch her. I wanted to trace the strap of her shirt over her shoulder and down her back. Her skin looked so smooth, so creamy that I almost needed to touch it just to make sure it was real. I wanted my tongue in that little hollow spot at the base of her throat and, for the first time, I wondered what she tasted like. What it would be like to kiss Woodstock. *Woodstock*!

She shouldn't look so good, all dressed for comfort, but she did. Way better than Alex in her skimpy skirts or Abby and Crystal at the party.

I jumped like a little girl when she clapped in front of my face. "Hello? Are you tired or something? You were totally spacing off for a minute there."

I shook my head. "I'm cool," I said, trying to play it off, when really, I was anything *but* cool right now. She shouldn't look so hot at this moment, but she did. Was this what love was? Thinking a girl looked beautiful in her pajamas and glasses? Glasses that I was probably one of the only guys she'd let see her wearing? Was that a good thing or a bad thing?

"Soooo? What movie did you want to watch?" she asked, her hands on her hips.

"Um, as long as it's not a romance, I'm game." I sat on her bed, my back against the headboard. I had enough to worry about in my own life to contemplate a happily ever after for two bad actors on a movie screen.

"Comedy?"

"Yep." I took a few deep breaths, trying to clear my head.

She put on some Will Ferrell movie and sat next to me on her bed. We'd done this a million times, leaned against this same headboard, our arms touching as we watched a movie, but it felt different. My skin tingled a little where she touched me. I was totally aware of that one spot more than I'd been aware of anything in my whole life. I didn't know if I wanted the feeling to go away or to feel it forever.

"So . . . I never said thanks for the other night." She dropped her head onto my shoulder. "God, I don't know what got into me. I was kind of nervous about something. I must have looked like such an idiot."

I put my arm around her. "Aw, don't worry about it. We've all gotten drunk and puked on a friend before. I think it's like a teenage rite of passage or something."

Her voice was soft when she spoke again. "Yeah, but I was going into a room with a guy I didn't even know, Bastian. What would have happened if you weren't there?"

I pulled her a little closer, trying to tell her that I would always be there. I hated it when girls got upset, especially Aspen, and all I wanted to do was make it better. "But I was. That's the whole point of the PPP. We watch out for each other."

She started picking at the peeled lettering on the old t-shirt I wore. When she found a stubborn piece, she pushed and her hand ended up touching my stomach through my shirt and I hissed, like I'd never been touched by a girl before. "You mean you watch out for us. You're always taking care of people, and I don't even think you realize it. Me, Jaden, Pris." Even though I didn't really believe a word she said, I let her keep going, enjoying what she said too much. "Do you think any other guy our age would have held my hair while I puked after ruining their favorite shirt? Carried their stupid, drunk friend up to their room and let them pass out in their bed while they slept in a chair? Nope. Just you."

"You might not think that if you knew I was hitting on a twin when you almost disappeared with that guy. I could have very easily screwed up and not been there when you needed me." I couldn't help it. Her skin was calling me too much. I was a guy and she was a girl, and that damn magnetic pull made me do it, but I rubbed my hand over her bare shoulder.

I did it softly, the way girls liked, whispering my fingers around the skin I'd been admiring. God she felt good. Why didn't other girls feel like this?

"But you still came. You bailed on that girl and found me when I needed you. You," she poked my side. It was such a friend move that I wanted to groan. Here I was savoring the feel of her and she was poking me. Nice. When did I turn into that guy? "Sebastian Hawkins, you are a caretaker. You'll never admit it, because you're too busy trying to be Mr. Ladies' Man, but you take care of people. Your mom . . . me . . ."

And there went the mood killer. "Pfft." I pulled away from her. "I do a pretty shitty job of taking care of my mom, Woodstock. You've seen her tears almost as much as me and now she has this new guy. I went out for lunch with them that day we were supposed to meet, and he was good. Played the perfect guy and even told me he wanted to marry her, but I don't even know if I can trust him." The floodgates were open and even though I'd regret this, I couldn't stop. "I kind of do, ya know? I think I want that normal life with two parents at home; but what if I do and he hurts her? I'm sick of not being able to protect her."

Aspen moved closer to me. We were facing each other now, her legs crossed in those stupid, sexy pajama bottoms. "She's your mom, Bastian. It's not your job to take care of her, and no matter if you trust the guy or not, she's the only one who can make her own decisions. And there's nothing wrong with wanting normal. You deserve it. You may be cocky and arrogant," she grabbed my hand, "but you deserve to have what you want. You deserve everything."

I wondered if she would still think that if she knew what I wanted was her. I tried to smile at her, before I eased back. I nodded my head and she settled in beside me again to watch the movie.

CHAPTER NINE

The rest of the week went by in a blur. DJ had taken me up on my offer, and I'd had to work every day straight until Friday came along. Lame. But at least I knew I'd have some extra cash flow when I got back, since I'd pulled some from my stash for the weekend. According to Pris, the house we had would be stocked with food, but I figured there'd be some stuff we'd want to do while we were there.

Speaking of cash, I took a quick break from my packing to pull up my Hook-up Doctor account. PA still hadn't been in contact with me. I was a little worried. Hopefully she hadn't had any problems and things were still on track. That fifty bucks would come in handy after this trip. Plus, I kind of hoped things turned out for her. Love was in the air and all that shit.

Because I'd decided that's what this was. I was in love. It kind of freaked me the hell out, but what could I do? Besides figure out my next step, which I needed to be doing. Did I want to believe Mom and go with all that fate and believing crap, or did I want to pretend I'd never taken a ride on the crazy train and try going back to the way things were? When I didn't think about kissing and touching Aspen every two seconds?

But then, I wasn't even sure I could do that.

When I saw one new message in my email folder, I clicked the little icon.

> *Hook-up Doctor,*
> *Can you tell I've been avoiding you? I screwed up. Big time.*

"Damn," I mumbled. I'd been afraid of this.

> *I thought I had a game plan in mind. When I got there, we talked a bit, but then went our separate ways. Then I saw him talking to another girl, and I got kind of bummed out. I know it's stupid, he's a guy and it was a party, but I lost my nerve. I figured if I drank a little bit, that might help me loosen up . . . Which totally isn't like me. Unfortunately, I got a little too loose.*

My body shot forward in the chair, like getting closer to the screen would make me read the message faster. I didn't know what it was, but something about this note felt familiar to me.

I got wasted. Like, way drunker than I've ever been. It was a mess. I flirted with the wrong guy, almost ended up locked in a room with him, puked, ruined a lucky shirt and had to get carried out of the party by my best friend!

My heart was thundering like crazy now. Was this what I thought it was? My leg bounced uncontrollably as I scrolled down.

I don't think puke is a real sexy look for a girl. I totally blew it. It's stuff like this that totally keeps you in the friend territory! I'm the girl who tried to be someone she wasn't, fell on her face and now, instead of noticing when I wear a really cute tank top and paint my nails, I'll be the funny one who vomited all over a party.

"Holy shit!" I jumped out of my chair. PA was Aspen. It had to be. The parties were the same night, she puked, got carried, ruined my lucky shirt. It all started making sense. All the little pieces of the pretty obvious puzzle I should have figured out much sooner started to fit together. I told PA to be extra nice to the guy and Aspen brought me job hunting. I told her to ignore him and she blew me off at the arcade. We talked at the party, separated and then I started talking with Crystal. She talked to the guy, saw me with a girl, and then got trashed.

"No freaking way." I ran a hand through my hair, all of a sudden feeling much better about this love thing than I had a few minutes ago.

The different clothes, the nails, the hair, all of it had been because she liked me. I was the chump! Okay, so it didn't sound as good when I said it that way, but we were friends. She'd said that in the beginning. That I liked girls who wore shirts too small and, well, not that I was real proud to admit it, but I guess Alex proved that theory, but hell, she wanted me.

She *wanted* me.

Aspen wanted me. I fell back into the chair, my head resting against the back. Suddenly, it was just excitement surging inside me. For some reason, it was a whole lot easier to accept it when I just wanted her, but knowing she felt the same made it real. What if she wanted to be my girlfriend? Considering she came to me—The Hook-up Doctor—to get together with, well, me, I was pretty sure that's exactly what she wanted.

I'd never done the girlfriend thing. Hell, I made fun of guys who did it at my age. But then, this was Aspen, and I'd just realized I loved her, so that should change things, right? Just five minutes ago, I hadn't been sure I wanted to go there, though. I'd never forgive myself if I did to her what countless guys had done to my mom.

Leaning forward, I started reading again.

How do I come back from this? Is it possible? And I can't believe I'm going to admit this to you, but since I don't know you, I figure it's okay. What if I start to have second thoughts?

No! My stomach dropped. Don't have second thoughts! "What did I do?" Damn, girls were confusing. I thought I had them figured out, but I was wrong. Three lines ago she liked me, and now, she wasn't sure!

Have you ever had girls contact you who thought they wanted one thing, but then kind

*of wondered about another? God, I'm such
a mess! Ignore that second thoughts part. I
just need your help. I can pay you overtime
or whatever since I'm the one who screwed
this up so badly. What should I do?*

PA Rocks

*P.S. Another what if. What should the girl
do if he still doesn't seem interested?*

I was definitely interested.

Even though I was practically shaking in my Vans, this changed everything. I was the freakin' Hook-up Doctor. Didn't I tell girls to decide who they were and stick with it? Well, it was time I decided who I was.

Flashes from the other night popped into my head: how her skin felt beneath mine while I touched her, talked to her. The protective rush I'd felt when that jackass tried to take her into the room. The cinnamon scent, and the way I loved how she looked all curled up in my bed. The rush I felt just hanging out with her. I'd never run in my whole life and sure didn't plan to start now.

I'd prove to her she wasn't stuck in the friend territory. That, even when she fell on her face, I'd pick her up again, and she didn't have to be anyone other than Woodstock for me. Mom would be proud. When it came to Aspen, I'd put every one of those cheesy romance books she read to shame. Watch out, world. The Hook-up Doctor was in love.

It was freaky how once you realized you loved someone, and they felt the same way about you, they could look different, yet the same; how they felt familiar, but not. As Aspen slept on my shoulder during the hour and a half drive to the beach, I realized a couple things. First, this whole love thing was confusing as hell. How *did* something look different, but still the same? It didn't make any sense at all. Yet, that was exactly how it felt. Good, but weird.

Second, Aspen really was one of the most gorgeous girls I'd ever seen. I'd apparently been pretty blind the past seventeen years, because she blew everyone else out of the water. She didn't even need the shiny nails or the tear drop necklace. She was perfect on her own.

And third, I was the biggest sap I knew.

I was imagining our weekend in my head. It wasn't frolicking through fields or anything, but pretty damn close. If Jaden could read my thoughts, I'd be done for. Like never coming back into my manhood, because of all the cheese-ball thoughts going through my head.

"I can't wait to get there. Your parents seriously rock, Pris." Jaden looked over at her from the passenger seat. "Puke-girl ruined our last epic weekend, so we're going to have to make up for it this time. Out of town girls are always hot."

"Is that all you think about? You drive me nuts." Pris narrowed her eyes at him before turning to look at the road again.

I closed my eyes while they argued in the front seat. I wasn't going to let anything ruin this weekend, and all their fighting ever did was put me in a bad mood. Right now, I just wanted to relax with Aspen.

Before I knew it, Pris pulled Aspen upright and Jaden was shaking me awake.

"We're here, sleeping beauty."

"Aw, thanks. I know I'm hot." I rubbed my sleepy eyes.

"Not you. You're the Beast. I was talking to Aspen." Jaden ripped the bag of chips from my lap and ran for the house. Idiot. Wasn't like I was going to chase him for some Cheetos.

Slowly, I climbed out of the car and stretched. The girls were grabbing their bags out of the trunk so I went over. "Here, let me help." I only had a small duffle bag on my back and my guitar in one hand, so I pulled Aspen's suitcase out with the other. Jaden came running back to help Pris. He wasn't as big of a jerk as he wanted people to think he was.

We followed the girls up the wooden stairs to the big, white two-story house. It was all old looking, but the girls were giggling over it and talking about how pretty it was, so I figured this was one of those things we didn't get about them. It wasn't that the house was torn up, but it definitely wasn't squeal-inducing, which is what they were doing right now.

Once she had the door open, we piled our way inside. "Nice," I said, scoping out the living room. The back wall was all windows, with a pretty quiet beach on the other side. I set the bags down on the hardwood floor.

"My parents have stayed here before," Pris said as she fell into the over-stuffed green chair. There was only the chair and a couch for furniture. Decent sized TV, a whole bunch of knick-knacks that I never really understood why people put out. It wasn't my style, but would definitely be a cool place to hang out at for the next few days.

"I still can't believe they rented this place for you. My mom is cool, but not *that* cool," I said.

Pris looked at the ground, her shoulders slumping. It was an un-Pris-like thing to do. "That's because she's not trying to get rid of you."

I crinkled my eyebrows, but before I could ask her what she meant, Aspen grabbed her hand and pulled her toward the stairs. "Let's go pick our rooms!"

"No way. We're in on this one. I'm not getting stuck with the crappy room." I jogged after them. Not one to be left behind, Jaden was right behind us. There was a bunch of clomping as we all raced to the top of the stairs. There were four doors in the hall, two on opposite sides at the very end and two closer to the stairs. We all headed for the back, everyone pushing to see who could get there first.

"Chill out, guys. It's Pris's birthday and her beach house. She gets first choice." Aspen grabbed onto my arm, and I stopped my pursuit of winning the killer room. Wow, this girl already had me wrapped around her fingers.

What was it with girls and the power they held over guys? Seriously, if this had happened a week before, I probably would have plowed my way through, given Pris the eyes and begged her until I got my way. Now, I found myself saying, "Woodstock is right. Pris chooses, then me."

128

"Hey!" Aspen bumped me with her hip, and I wanted to grab her there and pull her closer to me. "Whatever happened to ladies first?" It was strange. The little zing that went through me when she looked up at me with those big green eyes. It was at that moment I wondered why girls ever needed me—The Hook-up Doctor, I mean. If they all had the power she had in those eyes, they could have anything they wanted.

When I opened my mouth to reply, Pris cut me off. "You're mistaking them for real men, Aspen."

"Dude, what did I do?" Jaden asked. "I'm just standing here being all gentlemanly."

Pris rolled her eyes and mumbled something in Spanish. "I'm taking first choice, Aspen next and then you boys can argue over the last two rooms."

Just like I knew they would, the girls picked the two back rooms that looked out over the ocean, Pris on the right and Aspen on the left. I pushed past Jaden to try and call dibs on the better of the two leftover rooms, but he had the same idea. Luckily, I had way more skills than he did. Sticking my foot out, I tripped him up and reached for the other door on the left. Except, it wasn't a room. Jaden whooped from across the hall.

"Have fun sleeping in the bathtub, bro." He laughed, and I elbowed him.

There was no way I'd be sleeping in the damn bathroom. "Pris, I think we're missing a bedroom here."

"No, it just looks like it's a three bedroom house," she replied. "You know what they say about beggars."

Great. That would have been useful information before the trip. I leaned against the wall. "Why'd your parents get us a three bedroom place?"

"They didn't. They got me and Aspen a three bedroom house. You guys are crashing the party."

Shit. I'd forgotten about that. I looked over at Jaden. I really didn't want to share a room with him, but before I could say anything, he shook his head. "Nope. I need to have my space. Well, unless it's a girl doing the sharing, but not with you. Sorry, man."

"'Cause you're going to get lucky this weekend. Yeah, right."

At the same time Pris said, "You're not having a girl spend the night here with you!"

Ignoring what she said, I turned to the girls. "Can't you guys share a room and I can have the other one? It can be like a slumber party or whatever. You can put those weird masks on your faces and talk about how hot I am." They both narrowed their eyes at me. "What? I'm just sayin'."

"Have you ever tried to sleep in the same room with Pris? She snores like crazy. I'll be up all weekend." Aspen put her arm around Pris and pulled her closer. "I love you, girl, but you know it's true."

This weekend wasn't getting off to the start I wanted. "Okay, so my choices are the bathtub, living room, or sharing a room with Cupid over here who thinks he's getting some this weekend?"

Aspen sighed. "I guess I kind of owe you. I'll give up my room even though I really don't want to."

Like that was going to happen. I was raised by a single mom. Like I'd let a girl sleep on the couch, or put up with Pris's snoring. "Sometimes it sucks to be so damn sweet." I looked at Aspen. "You don't owe me, Woodstock. You can keep your stupid, oversized room with what is no doubt a really comfortable bed. I'll sleep downstairs."

Jaden laughed. "Sucks to be you."

"Do you always have to be a jerk?" Pris defended me, but I had a feeling it had less to do with me and more to do with her obvious anger at Jaden over something.

I turned to head for the stairs, but a cold hand on my arm stopped me. Then, somehow, it magically turned warm. Almost electric. "I have a King size bed in there. As long as you promise to be on your best behavior, you can share a room with me."

I froze. Every nerve ending in my body short circuited. Aspen wanted to share a room with me? *Ding, ding, ding. We have a winner*! I turned to face her. Pink tinted her cheeks. Man, I loved that look. Who would have thought blushing could be so sexy?

"I mean," she shrugged. "'Cause I owe you."

Deflate ego. It was an obligation thing. "I told you, you don't owe me," I snapped. The last thing a guy wanted to hear is that a girl wanted to share a room with him because she owed him.

"Okay, fine, not because I owe you, but just because . . . It's not a big deal, Bastian. I'm trying to be nice here. I don't have to have a reason." As her hand slid off me, I realized she hadn't let go earlier. I kind of missed her touch.

"You're sure?" I tried to play it cool, crossing my arms. "I mean, once we're in that room together it might hit you that you're sleeping in the same room with Sebastian Hawkins. I'm not sure many girl— ouch!" Aspen hit me. "I kid. I kid." *Mimicking* Borat would never get old. I think the movie came out when I was in elementary school, but to me it was a classic. "I think that bed will be much more comfortable than the bathtub. I'm in." *Yes!*

"Remember, best behavior?"

I raised my finger. "Scouts honor." Never mind I'd never been a Boy Scout in my life. I'd promise her anything right now.

CHAPTER TEN

"**D**ude, what's up with sharing a room with Aspen? You know that's going to seriously kill your chances of meeting any girls this weekend, don't you?" Jaden and I sat on the wooden steps of the front porch while waiting for the girls to get ready. It was still early, since we'd made sure to get up at the crack of dawn this morning when we left home.

I shrugged, fixing the buckle on my leather wrist band. "I doubt I would get any play in the bathtub, so I don't think I'm losing out on much." For some reason, my big mouth wanted to open and tell Jaden the whole truth. That I didn't want any other girl. That I'd rather chill in that room with Woodstock than have my mouth attached to any of the Alexes out there. There was sort of this line we didn't cross though. Jaden was my best guy friend, and I knew he'd always have my back, but we talked about hooking up, parties, piercing, video games and my lack of a vehicle. We didn't do the real stuff. I wasn't sure why. It wasn't that I thought he'd give me crap about it, but I guess I didn't want to be the one to go there first.

Jaden threw a glance over his shoulder. "Aspen . . . I can see why you wouldn't mind. Her and Pris, they're kind of better than the other girls out there, ya know?"

I stopped messing with my wristband and looked over at Jaden. His eyes were directed down at his foot while he slid it around on the step like he was rolling something. It was on the tip of my tongue to tell him he better get the idea of sharing a bed with Aspen out of his head, but something about the way his shoulders slumped made me keep my mouth shut. This wasn't Jaden territory. He didn't talk like this, so I knew something was up. "Yeah, we're lucky they put up with our shit."

"Huh. You can say that again."

This time, I was the one who looked behind us to make sure we were alone. I needed to tell someone, so I decided to just go for it. Who could you talk to if not your boy? "I like her, Jay. *Like-like her*. It has me a little freaked out. I don't want to mess it up."

He didn't laugh. Didn't smirk or ask me if I'd lost my mind. He actually kind of smiled at me. "You should go for it. It was only a matter of time 'til it happened, anyway. You guys will be like, the best couple ever!" He said the last part in a teasing, high-pitched voice. "Seriously though, you have my blessing, but if you hurt my little girl, I'm pulling out the shotgun."

I laughed. "Thanks for letting me date your daughter. I'm sure she'll be surprised to find out she's your love child." Jaden held out his fist, and I bumped it with mine. After a minute of silence, I asked, "What about you? You ready to change your ways and settle down with the old ball and chain?"

The Jaden I'd known for years looked up at me and smirked. "Nah, I'm not that crazy. Too many girls out there to tie myself to one." I laughed, even though something in his voice didn't sound right. The screen door slammed as the girls came out, keeping me from asking him what was wrong.

We headed out on foot since the town was about the size of my shoe. Okay, maybe I'm exaggerating. From what I heard, it was a pretty popular spot for the college crowd to hang out. We went into a few shops, which I fought not to roll my eyes at. The girls liked this kind of crap, so this was me trying to be sensitive to what Aspen liked. Even though I knew she already liked me too, it couldn't hurt to score some extra points in the sensitivity department, since I knew it wasn't my strong point.

They looked at so many dolphin and ocean pictures, jewelry, the little knickknack-y things that were in the beach house, and who knew what else, for so long that I nearly fell asleep walking, but unlike Jaden, I didn't complain once. I was whipped already. Funny, I didn't even care. Not too much, at least . . .

After what felt like years, we found an all-ages pool hall to eat lunch in.

I pulled up the chair by Aspen and tried to sit down, but Pris leapt between me and the seat and plopped down. O-kay. Obviously, she didn't want to sit by Jaden. He was ruining my game with whatever was going on between him and Pris.

After everyone decided what they wanted, I offered, "I'll get Aspen and Pris's food when I order mine." When three pairs of eyes devoured me, I added, "Pris's birthday meal and all." I didn't want to look like an idiot. Was I trying too hard? This was tougher than I thought.

"That doesn't mean you need to buy mine." Aspen moved to stand up, but I put my hand on her shoulder.

"I want to. Sit down, Woodstock, before I tie you to the chair."

She glanced over at Pris, before turning back to me. "I just want the chicken strips, fries and a coke."

"Same for me, Bastian. Thanks." Pris looked at Jaden and rolled her eyes. Okay, there was definitely something weird going on there. They never got along particularly well. It was one of those strange friendships where you knew they were close, just as close as the rest of us, but they never showed it. They never agreed on anything, and lately, it was even worse.

"What, you're not going to buy mine? That's janky." Jaden stood up and followed me. I ordered my burger and the girls' chicken before Jaden ordered his.

"Here," Jaden handed me five bucks. "This is for Pris's."

Huh? Why didn't he just say that at the table? "Okay." I took the money.

"Don't tell her though." My only reply was to nod my head. There was definitely something going on here.

We stood up front until they called out our number, and then brought the food back to the table.

Unfortunately, I couldn't enjoy my meal.

"Dude, those guys need to stop watching our table." I nodded my head at the two standing by the corner

138

pool table. They looked about our age. Preppy looking guys in polo shirts.

Everyone at my table turned to look, and I realized my mistake. Pris and Aspen hadn't seen the guys eyeing them, and now, they obviously did. I mean, I knew I was the shit, but that didn't mean I wanted to introduce Aspen to anyone who might be my competition. Not that they would really be competition, anyway.

"What? It's okay for the two of you guys to drool over girls, but not okay for guys to look at us?" Pris asked in her best I-am-woman-hear-me-roar voice.

I felt my brows crinkle as I looked at her. *Exactly, because now I like Aspen and realize it's pretty annoying.* Okay, so maybe not. I mean, I still didn't want guys scoping out my girl, but I guess it probably did get frustrating when Jay and I hit on girls around them. "So we won't do it again if we get to kick a guy's ass if they start panting over you girls." See? Compromise. I'd heard that was good for relationships.

"Speak for yourself, man." Jaden took a drink of his soda. Both girls rolled their eyes, before Pris grabbed Aspen's arm.

"Come on, Aspen. Let's go play pool." They

started to walk away. Aspen looked over her shoulder and gave me half a smile and shrugged like she was saying sorry. My feet itched to walk to them, but the last thing I wanted to look like was creepy-stalker-boy. This whole thing was so much harder than hooking up. I wasn't used to caring about guys checking out a girl. Caring if they walked over to play a game of pool about twenty feet from idiots on the prowl. I knew that look. Hell, I'd had that look, and I didn't want it steered toward Aspen. Either of the girls really, but Pris for a totally different reason.

And now it was pretty clear to me why I'd always played The Hook-up Doctor rather than love connection. It sucked.

I watched as Pris racked the balls. That's when it happened. Aspen bent over to shoot the ball and yeah, I had a perfect view. It was like angels singing. The sky opened up, and that ray of light pointed right at her. Okay, maybe not like that, because it's cheesy as hell, but still . . . I know I realized I loved her now, but I was still a guy. I don't care how much guys denied or how much girls didn't want to think about it, we're visual creatures. It's hard not to admire a girl, especially when you actually liked her. Personally, I thought it was pretty damn cool. To enjoy talking to a girl, wanting to hold her hand and also silently thanking God when she bent over and you got a glimpse of her curves.

No matter how whipped I was, I'd obviously still be a guy. That gave me some relief.

"You're drooling." Jaden nudged the elbow I was leaning on, making it fall off the table.

"Shut up." Lame reply, but it was all I had. I shot forward in my chair. Preppy loser boys were walking over to the girls. I pushed to my feet, but Jaden pulled me back to the chair again. "What the hell, dude?"

Jaden laughed. "Easy there, big guy. You haven't even told her you like her. You don't even know if she likes *you*, Bastian."

"She does." I was fully aware that I sounded like I was five years old. So sue me.

"And how's that? Because you're Sebastian Hawkins?" He laughed again.

Since I couldn't tell him I was The Hook-up Doctor and Aspen contacted me to hook her up with . . . well, me, I ignored him.

I looked at him, all leaned back in his chair like he didn't have a care in the world. That was supposed to be *me*. When did I become the guy all stressed out because he wanted a girl and didn't know what to do? My entire way of living had been totally knocked off-track and screwed-up, but also made more sense than it ever had, at the same time. "Don't be an asshole."

"I'm not. I'm just sayin'. You go over there all me-Tarzan-my-woman before she even knows you're into her, and you're going to look like an ass. You need to chill. They're just talking."

My best friend was really pissing me off. When the hell did he start making sense? I was supposed to be the teacher, not the student. "Fuck you."

Jaden pulled out his cell phone and looked at it. "We'll give them like ten minutes, go over and say we gotta go or something. Then, you need to get down on one knee, or whatever it is you're planning on doing, before you seriously ruin our weekend."

I raked both my hands through my hair. "Arg. Eight minutes and not a second longer." And then just because we'd kind of changed the dynamic of our friendship today and because Jaden had somehow become smarter than me when it came to girls, I said, "Thanks."

We fist bumped again, because it was much manlier than getting sappy twice in one day. For eight whole minutes, we were nothing but silent. I watched the douche-bags talk to the girls. Pris was laughing a lot, leaning closer to them the way I might instruct her to do if she were a client and they were her potential hook-up. Woodstock smiled a few times, obviously not as interested in them as Pris was, but she still looked to be enjoying herself.

Jerks.

Jaden kicked my foot to signal eight minutes was up. As soon as I got to my feet, my boy was by my side. I tried not to rush too much to reach them. "You guys ready to go?" I asked, being sure to stand next to Aspen. So, I was jealous and pretty much marking my territory. If I wasn't so annoyed, I'd probably be laughing at myself, right now.

"Sure," Aspen replied while at the same time Pris said, "No."

"Come on, Priscilla," Jaden mumbled, using her whole name. It was almost enough to distract me. We never called Pris by her real name.

Pris changed her weight from one foot to the other. "We're planning a party with Jason and Ron. We figured it would be fun to have some people over."

It was so strange, because just a week ago, this would have been what I wanted. Parties meant girls, and I'd have been all for that. Now, I couldn't stop thinking about how drunken guys would try and hit on Aspen all night. I just wanted to chill with her, so I could find that perfect moment to tell her that I liked her the way she liked me. "I thought we'd hang out the four of us tonight, Pris. You know, celebrate your birthday with your best friends."

Jaden leaned against the pool table. "I'm all for the party."

I knew, no matter what I said, this party was happening. Out of instinct, I put my arm around Aspen, but then something came out of my mouth that was very deliberate. "Our room is off limits to anyone but us. I plan on enjoying it." Now, there'd be no question in these guys' minds that this girl was off-limits. Of course, my statement also made it sound like there was something kinky going on, which I didn't really mean. I meant enjoy the room because I would, but if they drew their own conclusion . . .

Aspen pushed me.

She cut her eyes at me. "*My* room, Bastian. I'll have anyone I want in my room." Aspen turned to Pris, and the jerks were smirking like they'd hit the damn jackpot, and I wanted nothing more than to pummel them.

"Invite who you want and text us later, okay?" Pris

said to one of them. They hugged the girls and then walked out.

"You guys can be suck jerks." Pris grabbed Aspen's arm, and then the two of them stalked out.

I groaned. I'd obviously screwed up. "What the hell just happened?"

Jaden shook his head at me like he felt sorry for me. "And now you know why I'm sticking to hook-ups. Girls are crazy."

This weekend wasn't going the way I'd imagined it. The girls managed to avoid us for the rest of the day. They went to the store to pick up stuff for the party that I was still totally against. Who would have thought it? Sebastian Hawkins didn't want to party. Once I decided to go for it with Aspen, I wanted this weekend to be special. You know, like long walks on the beach, and all that other special stuff that used to make me want to gouge my own eyes out.

They spent the afternoon locked in Pris's room getting ready. Jaden tried to hang out, but I wasn't really in the mood. I spent some time playing my guitar before getting ready. Whether I approved or not, I still planned to look damn good. I wore a pair of long, khaki shorts that went below my knees, black Vans, and a black button up shirt.

When I got downstairs, Jay wasn't there, but the girls were sitting on the porch. As I walked out to talk to them, the jerks from the pool hall showed up with a few cases of beer in their hands. *Great.* Before I could get a chance to try and talk to Aspen, Tweedle Dee and Tweedle Dum pulled the girls inside. A few minutes later a couple more guys showed up. Girls, guys, girls, guys, in flocks until the house looked like some frat party I should be enjoying much more than I was. We didn't even have time to come up with our Pre-party Plan. *And I sound like a freakin' idiot.*

Was it possible love screwed with your head? I mean, girls didn't realize the power they held. That they were really the ones who pulled the strings. Even when we thought we had the power, it was them, because right now I had a hot chick shaking what her mama gave her in my face, and all I could think of was Aspen, and if she was mad at me or not, and how we'd make it through a hell of a good party without a PPP.

"Hi." A warm body pressed against me, and it felt all wrong. Flowers, not the damn cinnamon that was driving me to the nut house.

"Hey." I moved away from her through the crowd of people filling the beach house.

"What's your name?" Great. The leech was still on my tail.

"Sebastian."

"Do you want to dance or something?"

I sighed, stopped and looked at her. It surprised me, because she didn't look like the girls who usually approached me at parties. She dressed like Aspen would instead of flashing the goods to everyone. It was a nice change, but as nice as it was, she wasn't who I needed right now. "I really appreciate you asking, but I'm kind of looking for my girl. I mean, she's not mine, but I'm hoping she will be. Well, she's my friend, but I like her, and she's pissed at me." *Ding. Ding. Ding.* Somebody call the fight, because it has ended. I'd officially lost my touch. Here I was *rambling* about a girl to a *girl*.

I'd given Aspen, AKA PA, shit about rambling the first time we talked, and here I was doing the same thing. "I'm sorry, but I gotta go." *Drown myself in the ocean*. Not really, but I felt like it. This situation was so fucked up, I couldn't believe it.

I pushed my way through the house and went out the back door. People were already congregating outside, but closer to the house, so I stomped through the sand until the blackness of the ocean was right in front of me, and I could taste the salt in the air.

"Come out here to make me feel like one of your playthings again?" Aspen sat on a rock about fifteen feet away from me. The sharpness in her voice stung me.

And I also had no idea what the hell she was talking about.

"Um, English, please?"

Aspen crossed her arms and turned away from me. Uh-oh. That meant trouble. I walked over to her, a smile curving my lips for the first time since the Tweedle bothers showed up. "Woodstock . . . come on." I stepped in front of her, knowing all I needed to do was get her to look at me and all would be forgiven. She turned away. "Hey. Stop avoiding me." I stepped up right next to her. Her hands were over her face now, blocking her from me. "Aspen, talk to me."

Her hands jerked away. "That's exactly what I'm talking about! You're treating me like one of your little girls. You totally made me sound like some hooker who was sharing a room with you in more than just a friendly way, but who would try and talk to other guys. Now you're using the smooth voice. Trying to wrap me around your finger, but I'm pissed, so think again, buddy!" She poked my chest and tried to walk away, but I grabbed her wrist gently.

"Hey." I almost shook my head at how my voice sounded. It wasn't that smooth voice I used on other girls, it was emotional, sincere. "I would never treat you badly. You should know that."

She looked up at me with big eyes, and I could tell that I'd somehow hurt her much more than I realized. I was still a little lost on how, but I intended to figure that out. "Let's go for a walk?"

She nodded her head yes, so I let my hand slide down her wrist until it latched with hers, twining our fingers together. And it didn't feel like I was trying to brand her, it didn't feel crazy and obsessive, it just felt good.

I led her down the beach, trying to walk slow and easy when my whole body felt jacked up on adrenaline. Neither of us spoke until we were pretty far from that house. I stopped her. "I didn't mean to make you sound like a hooker." But I sounded like an idiot. "How did I do that exactly?"

Aspen sighed, but she didn't let go of my hand. "Bastian, you made it sound like we were hooking-up or something. It just sucked. I know there's nothing really going on with us, but I don't like feeling like some name on your list."

Did I say I was jacked up on adrenaline? Now it felt closer to cardiac arrest. I was slipping. Totally losing it, scared to do what I wanted. Freaked out because this time it was something totally different and if I screwed it up, it would kill me.

But the thing was . . . I'd never backed down before, and I didn't plan to start now. "What if there was?" I hooked my finger under her chin, so she couldn't look away from me.

It took her a few seconds to reply and when she did, she sounded all breathy. Just how I felt. "What if there was what?"

"Something going on between us," I said, and lowered my lips to hers.

CHAPTER ELEVEN

So, yeah. You know how when you're watching one of those romance movies and the girl and guy kiss for the first time and the skies split open and doves or something like that are sent down from Heaven to grace them? A love song plays in the background, and the kiss looks perfect? They both move together like they've been doing it forever, and every girl in the audience says, "aww" in unison?

I didn't hear the music. The sky was still dark and the birds were asleep for the night, but I had no doubt if we had a crowd of teen girls they'd be oohing and awing because we didn't need any of that extra shit. It felt perfect, and I knew it had to look perfect, because it just felt right.

There was the second of hesitancy when we first touched that her soft lips tensed—probably in shock—but then they relaxed, and molded against mine. That cinnamon scent of hers floated around me, but I tasted it, too, all spicy and Aspen, going straight to my head. How could I not have kissed her before? It was like my first time. Actually, I'm pretty sure it was because kissing other girls didn't feel like this.

When she pulled her arms up and wrapped them around my neck, and I felt her body press against mine, everything inside me started to pop and explode. I teased her lips with my tongue, and she opened up to let me inside. It felt like static electricity—the little zap as her tongue tangled with mine. When she weaved her fingers through the back of my hair, I moaned. I *hated* it when girls put their hands in my hair, but this wasn't just a girl. It was Aspen.

And just like that, it was over.

"Whoa!" She jerked away, walking in a circle. "Wow. I mean, what was that?"

I don't know where it came from. Maybe the high of kissing her for the first time made me a little delirious or something, but I chuckled. "I think that's supposed to be my line."

Her arms were wrapped around herself as she looked at me. "Sebastian, we just kissed! And it was . . ." She stopped walking, opening her mouth, and closing it again.

"I left ya speechless, huh?"

She punched me in the arm. "How can you be conceited at a time like this? You're my best friend,

Bastian. We can't do this," she waved her arm back and forth between us. "I'm not one of your girls. I'm not going to think I won the jackpot because Sebastian Hawkins stuck his tongue down my throat, and then broke my heart by never talking to me again."

Okay, that dented my high a bit. "What? I'm not like that. The girls I hook-up with are in it just for fun. I don't break hearts, Woodstock, and you know it. Not after . . ." *My mom.* She knew I'd never let a girl think our relationship was more than it was.

She collapsed into the sand, still looking a little out of it. "I know. Sorry, I'm just . . ." Aspen locked her hands behind her head. Then she sighed, sliding her hand down and touching her fingers to her lips. "You kissed me. I mean, lately things have been different, and I've thought about it, but I never thought it would happen. I wasn't even sure how I—but you did. And it was . . ."

I fell down beside her. "Hot."

Aspen laughed and the little ball of stress that was starting to form in my chest loosened. "That's not the word I was going to use, but kind of." She buried her face in her hands. "Holy crap."

"Hey." I pulled her hands away. I turned so I faced her, sitting cross-legged in the sand. Woodstock did the same. "I don't want you to feel like this is

153

something less than what it is. This is . . ." Damn, this was kind of hard. None of my knowledge about the opposite sex prepared me for this moment. I knew all about helping people hook-up, but how did you tell a girl that you liked her? That you loved her, and you wanted to be with her because she was so much better than all those other girls out there? Girls could do that. They could talk and go on and freaking on about their feelings, but with guys, it was like this little box of mixed up thoughts locked inside my head. The words were there, but I didn't know how to get to them. I'd try and make sense of them, to unlock the box, but then it would slam shut, and all those words would be a jumbled mess again.

"We're different. I mean, I want to be different with you. I like you, Woodstock. Almost sent me to the psych ward when I first realized it. Since when did I actually *like* a girl, much less my best friend? Freaked me out, but I do. Like you and want you, I mean." *I totally suck at this.*

"Um, thanks, I think?"

"Argh!" I rubbed my hand over my face. "That was lame, but just focus on the part where I said I like you. More than anything, Aspen." I reached out and touched her face. The beach around us was completely dark except for a few lights scattered along the sidewalk about a hundred feet behind us. The black water lapped up the shore, closer and closer to us, but we didn't move. "You're so soft. How did it take me so long to figure that out?"

Her eyes closed, and she leaned her cheek into my hand. "I've liked you forever, Bastian. For years I imagined us being together, but you never seemed to feel the same. I was finally moving on."

I had no idea what the moving on part was about, because I knew she hadn't moved on from me. I had my Hook-up Doctor emails to prove that, but I didn't want to embarrass her. I didn't want her to know that I knew what she did, and that I was The Hook-up Doctor, so I just said, "I'm showing you now. I'm going crazy for you, Aspen."

This time it was her who leaned forward, taking my mouth. This kiss was even hotter than the last one. She crawled toward me. I threaded my fingers through her hair, pushing her head closer to me. That zinging was back inside me, ricocheting around like a pinball. I wanted to touch her, but didn't want to move too fast. We were both on thin ice, and the last thing I wanted to do was push her. But God, as she deepened the kiss, I couldn't help it. I swear I tried to be strong, but everything inside me was calling to her.

I leaned forward, laying her back against the sand. Aspen went easily. I rested my body on top of hers. Just touching her like this. Holding her face as our bodies touched everywhere made me feel like a freakin' rock star.

After what could have been two minutes or two years, I made the good guy inside me win the tug-o-war and pulled away. Man, I wanted her, but I didn't want her to think it was all physical. I lay down beside her in the sand. Aspen leaned her head on the crook of my arm, so I wrapped it around her. I wanted to jump for joy, but I was too cool for that.

"I'm in shock," she whispered. One of her arms fell over my chest, and her hand tickled my hair.

"Must be a side effect of my amazing kissing skills," I teased her.

"Oh, yeah. Must be," sarcasm dripped from her words.

Without the playfulness in my words, I spoke, "I don't want to mess this up. I know this might come as a surprise to you, but I've been known to make a mess of things."

"No? You?" *Tickle. Tickle.* I actually kind of loved having my hair played with now.

"Like I said, a shock, huh?" It rocked that she got my sense of humor and always dished it right

156

back at me. I breathed deep, trying to slow the drum solo that was my heartbeat. *You can do this, Bastian.* I needed to get real for just a second. I wanted to make sure she knew that this was different. That I loved her, even though I'd probably drop dead swallowing my tongue if I tried to tell her. Those three words? Scary as hell. Maybe not for people who threw them around, but for a guy who never expected to feel them and did? Yeah, they pretty much made me want bury my head in the sand and never come up.

But if I wanted to be good to her, really good, make her and my mom proud, I needed to say *something.* I pulled her on top of me. Her legs were on either side of me, straddling me as I felt the water rising enough to touch my Vans. She was worth ruining a pair of shoes over.

"You're freaking me out, Bastian. You look like you're about to puke."

Great. I totally sucked at this knight-in-shining-armor thing. "The other night at your house you said I want to take care of people. That I want to protect people? Just you, Woodstock. The only people in this world I need to protect are my mom and you."

She smiled, and I squeezed her tighter. That hadn't been so hard. Maybe this would work out after all.

"It's not just your kissing that's amazing, Bastian. It's you."

The next morning I woke up with a body pressed tight against mine. We'd stayed at the beach talking—okay, and kissing (but that's it, I swear) for most of the night. When we were pretty sure the party had died down, we went back to the house. Pris was kicking the stragglers out and, after about five minutes of girl talk between them in the kitchen in which I heard some squealing, Aspen and I had gone up to bed. To my surprise, on our way up, we found Jaden all tucked in with the blanket up to his chin like his mommy had put him to bed.

It was strange. Jaden was almost always the last to leave a party, but at the time, I hadn't been able to give it much thought. I'd had Aspen's hand in mine, and I was going to have her in my arms all night. Kind of distracted me from anything else. It was pretty shocking I could even think straight.

Now, I was distracted by something else. I really didn't want her to know how much I wanted her and with the way I was holding her, if she woke up, she'd definitely know. Really, it's not my fault though; she's hot, and I'm a guy. It's physics or something like that. So, I tried the old swift roll move I heard about, casually moving away from the way her back tucked against my front. It was a crappy situation. I definitely didn't want to leave her, but I didn't want her to think I was a perv either.

When I got out of the shower and made it back to the room, she sat on the pale yellow blanket, with bed head and shy eyes.

"Hey." She looked all apprehensive, like she thought I'd changed my mind since last night or something. I needed to reassure her, but also wanted to try and keep things light. Last night was heavy enough, and it might be a news flash, but I wasn't real into heavy.

"Who would have thought pillow hair could be so sexy? I don't know if I want to kiss you, or hand you a brush!"

Her mouth tilted up into a smile. I couldn't help but return it. "You're such a nutcase." She tossed a pillow at me, but I grabbed her hand when she swung, pulling her toward me.

"Definitely kiss you."

Her hand snaked up between us, she grabbed my shirt. *Yes!* Then pushed me away. *No!*

"Gross. I probably have morning breath!" She covered her mouth with her hand and then ran from the room. Girls . . .

159

When I got downstairs to the kitchen, Jaden and Pris were both there. Pris fingered a necklace around her neck, that weird Jaden/Pris tension was thick in the air. "So, how'd the party go last night?" I asked, flopping down into a chair.

"Fine," they both answered in unison. *O-kay.*

"Plans today?" I grabbed a piece of toast off Pris's plate and popped a bite in my mouth. "Thanks."

"You're lucky I love you, Bastian, but I still have to warn you, you hurt her and you're going down. That's all I have to say."

I sat forward and touched Pris's arm. "Hey, I'm not going to hurt her. I think I'm in love with her." Pris's fork dropped, clinking against her plate. Jaden started choking on the other side of the table. Probably wasn't real cool to tell Pris and Jay before I told Aspen, but I wanted Pris to know that I wouldn't hurt Aspen. Yeah, I'm a wuss. I can't help it.

"So, what are we doing today?" Aspen came around the corner and into the kitchen. I pulled my hand away from Pris.

"That's what I'm trying to figure out, too."

CHAPTER TWELVE

"Are you sure about this, Sebastian?" Aspen asked as we stood on the edge of the dense forest. We'd done the town thing the day before. I didn't want to tell her, but if I went into one more shop we wouldn't make it out without me throwing a much bigger fit than Jaden had. Hence, my whole idea about exploring. Of course, I was no Grisly Adams. I didn't plan to get myself lost, but I figured we could look around a little bit without ending up on the nightly news as one of those groups of people who wandered off and were never seen again.

Plus, there were trails. I made sure.

I pulled her close to me just because I could. "Aw, I'll take care of you, baby. I promise."

She got that cute pink on her cheeks and she gave me the biggest smile I'd ever seen. Made me feel like the man, knowing I could make her look like that. I put my lips to hers because I didn't think I'd ever get tired of her. "I'll be like your bodyguard or something. Me Tarzan. You Jane."

"I think I'm going to puke," Jaden mumbled. Pris pushed him before I had a chance to tell him he was just jealous.

"I wasn't really thinking bodyguard. More like tour guide." Aspen rolled her eyes playfully.

I grabbed her hand as we all headed down the trail. "That, too. I can do it all." I winked at her.

It was actually pretty cool. I wasn't really the type who got all "one with nature." We usually left that stuff up to Mama and Daddy Peace, but it was chill out there. Pris and Jaden kept the arguing to a minimum, Aspen kept herself glued to my side, and there were birds and trees and rustling leaves and all that stuff. It felt like one of those long walk on the beach moments. Cheesy to think about, but actually cool when you really did it.

"Shh. Look," Aspen whispered. My feet stopped dead on the brush covered ground, maybe slightly scared she saw a big bear or something, but I'd never admit it. Luckily it was just two little squirrels both trying to get the same pinecone. I exhaled. I could take a squirrel much easier than a bear if need be.

"Awww," both girls sighed.

It made me laugh. All it took was Chip and Dale to get them acting all girly.

We did a little more exploring, even finding an old

cave that I'm not afraid to admit freaked me out a little bit. Luckily, it was pretty open so we had enough light to peek around.

"Boo!" Jaden grabbed Pris's waist and she screamed, then proceeded to kick his ass. While they were engaged in World War Five Hundred, I took advantage and snuck Aspen into a dark corner, hoping I didn't get attacked by a killer bat or something.

My hands found their home on her hips, and I pulled her toward me. "I think I'm addicted to you. Now that I know I can kiss you and touch you, I don't want to stop."

"I bet you tell all the girls that," she teased.

"What girls? There aren't any other girls, but you."

Her arms wrapped around my neck. They felt good there. "You're good at this."

"I'm a natural." I don't know if she was going to reply, because I kissed her again. It was slow, and smooth. Not rushed, but definitely hot. I let my lips slide down her chin, to her neck. Her skin tasted so sweet that it pulled a groan from the back of my throat. Who would have known kissing someone you love was so much better than kissing other girls? Slowly, I slipped my fingers under the bottom of her shirt, brushing my thumb along the smooth skin of her side. I just liked touching her, savoring the little zing that I got from being skin to skin with her.

"Dude, if you guys wanted to get busy, all you had to do is ask for some privacy." Now I understood why Aspen and Pris were always telling Jaden to shut up.

"I second that."

I stepped away from Aspen. "Well at least we found something you two can agree on." I gave both Pris and Jaden hard looks. "Let's go get some lunch."

After they started to walk away, I stopped Aspen. "It wasn't a line."

"I know. I trust you, Bastian."

Her words made me stumble a little bit. That was a heavy burden, someone completely putting their trust in you. But I loved her, and that would make everything okay. She could trust me. I'd find a way to make sure I earned it.

I lay in the bed with Aspen curled beside me wondering why the hell I'd ever made fun of guys who were whipped. Okay, so those guys who got whipped over every girl needed to get a life, but when it was the right girl, you'd have to be an idiot not to get whipped. I mean, I had this great girl. She was funny, smart, hot, gave me shit *and* I could touch her, kiss her, hold her, and lay with her any time I wanted. She looked at me like I hung the friggin' moon. It made me feel invincible. Like the luckiest seventeen-year-old guy in the world. Why wouldn't I want to do anything for her? Want to be with her all the time? Despite popular belief, I wasn't stupid.

After lunch, we'd come back to the house. Jaden and Pris were off at separate ends of the house, and I was cuddled up with my girl. If this was being whipped, chain me up, baby!

A couple hours later, I gently rubbed Aspen's shoulder. She slept like the dead. I couldn't do more than an hour nap even with her body against mine. I'd gone downstairs to hang out with Jaden and Pris for a while. When we got tired of waiting for her, I offered to go upstairs and wake her up to go swimming. "Come on sleepy head. Time to get up. The beach is calling our names."

I changed into my swimming shorts in our room while Aspen and Pris got changed in her room. I'd now been sitting downstairs with Jaden for thirty minutes, and they still weren't out yet. Don't ask me why it took so long to put on a swimming suit, but we were both getting antsy so we went ahead and headed out, figuring they'd find us easy enough. On the way out, I made sure to grab both mine and Aspen's beach towels because I was sweet like that.

After laying them both out on the sand, fixing the corner so it was just right, I walked over to Jaden who was eyeing me like I had ten heads or something. "What?"

"Dude, you are so messed up."

Okay, so I had two choices right now. I could just blow Jaden off because I knew he was wrong and it didn't really matter what he thought. Or I could give it to him straight. I wasn't really the quiet type. Sure, I knew he was just surprised to see me like this and that a few weeks ago, I would have been the same way if the situation was reversed, but . . . I guess you could say I'd been enlightened and I wouldn't be me if I didn't rub that in his face just a little. I'd expect the same thing out of him. We were guys and that's just how guys roll.

So I told him what was up. "You went to bed alone last night, Jay. I held a girl all night. I'll do it again tonight. She likes it when I kiss her; she kisses me, and on top of that, she's a seriously kickass girl. She doesn't play games, isn't out there making out with a different guy every weekend. Just me. If that's messed up, I'm there, bro."

Jaden threw his hat at me. "Still trying to figure out why she'd want to kiss your ugly mug."

"Because I have skills. One day, I'll pass that

knowledge on to you." I threw his hat down and ran out to the water. Jaden was right behind me. As soon as we were waist deep, he splashed my face, so I tackled him and tried to drown his ass. "Don't start a fight you can't win."

"Please, I can take you!" We kept going after each other—we took our competitions seriously, even if they were just with water—until I heard a whistle from the beach.

"Will you guys ever grow up?" I turned toward Pris's voice. My heart nearly stopped when I saw Aspen standing next to her.

"Ho-ly shit."

"You can say that again," Jaden said from beside me.

That snapped me out of my visual pleasure for a minute. "Don't look at my girl, asshole."

"I'm not."

"Have they worn bikinis every summer?" I asked.

"No clue, but I'm glad they are now."

Pris and Aspen stood with their feet in the water. I took my eyes off Woodstock just for a second. Red, Pris wore a red bikini, but it was nothing compared to the turquoise gift from God that Aspen wore. The dark blue was a nice contrast to the creamy white of her skin. It looked like some kind of Hawaiian pattern with white flowers scattered on the blue material. It was the most I ever remembered seeing of her body. I liked the view: a nice stomach, curvy hips and legs, man the girl had nice legs. *Humina, humina, humina.*

I knew my eyes were probably bulging out of my head, but I didn't care. My whole body, and I do mean whole body, came alive at the sight of her. She was gorgeous.

"Still think I'm messed up?" I asked Jaden as they started walking in the water toward us.

When he didn't reply, I glanced at him. Jaden's mouth was still hanging open. I laughed and headed toward Aspen, meeting her halfway.

Playing with Aspen in the water was way better than beating Jaden in a splash contest. We spent hours out there messing around. I'm not going to lie and say I didn't dunk her, because whipped or not, I still liked to have a little fun. She loved it though, splashing around and playing like she needed to be rescued after I'd pull her under the water. The rescuing was fun . . .

Then we floated together, riding the waves and holding onto each other, salt tinged her skin when I kissed her.

Hot.

* * *

"Building a fire should not be that difficult, guys." Aspen laughed at Jaden and me as we messed around trying to get the fire pit going.

"It's not me. Jaden keeps screwing it up." I nudged my friend with my shoulder.

"Dude, I'm the one who said douse the thing with lighter fluid. That will get it going." Jaden fell onto one of the blankets, obviously handing the reins over to me. Good. I'd get it done faster without him, anyway. Once I had red flames popping and cracking in the pit, I smirked at Jaden, before joining Aspen on our pallet, pushing my guitar over to give me room to sit down.

"You warm enough, baby?" I asked her. Funny how one little phrase can ignite reactions faster than my blazing fire. Aspen blushed, Pris sighed, and Jaden snorted. Whatever. I only cared about one response. She nodded as I sat down beside her.

The sun slipped behind the ocean a few minutes later, so we went ahead and roasted some hotdogs on the fire for dinner. It was our last night here, so Aspen and I managed to talk Jaden and Pris into a truce of sorts so we could spend the night together. The beach was dead, leaving nothing but flames, waves, a dark night, and the four of us.

"What do you guys want to do?" Aspen asked. I sat

behind her, with her between my legs, her back against my chest. I squeezed her tighter trying to tell her that I just wanted to be close to her. Pris looked over at Jaden, their blankets were beside each other, while Aspen and I shared one.

"Hey, remember that time we all went camping with Aspen's parents?" Pris asked.

"Dude, so glad we didn't end up with tofu dogs this time." Jaden laughed.

"What was that story her dad told us? Remember the claw man or whatever and this punk over here," Pris tossed a glance at Jaden, "decided to try and scare us in the middle in the night."

"Try? You screamed like a little girl."

"That's not because we thought you were the claw man! It's because you freaked out when you thought you heard a bear and got tangled in our tent! Try being asleep when your tent falls on top of you, with a *screaming boy* thrashing around in it!" I felt Aspen's laugh vibrate my chest as she spoke.

"There were bear warnings on the damn table! How was I supposed to know Aspen's parents were going to be outside being all one with nature, in the woods, in the middle of the night? Her dad's big. He could pass for a bear." Jaden mumbled the last part.

"Oh, yeah!" I laughed. "Daddy Peace with his

tie-dyed shirts and peace and love attitude could totally pass for a bear. Scary. You almost pissed your pants, Jay."

"My life, like, flashed before my eyes and shit." You could hear the pout in his voice.

I don't know where it came from, but I felt the urge to keep talking. Jaden was my boy and even though I gave him shit like the girls, I also gave props where props were due. "He was scared, but as soon as he fought his way through the tent, the first thing he told me was to get the bear's attention so we could steer him away from you guys." I kissed Aspen on top of the head. She squeezed my hand in return. Everyone was quiet for a minute, until I spoke again. "Would have been a good plan if we didn't accidently run Aspen's mom down when we tried to save you girls."

We all started laughing. It felt good, holding my girl and laughing with my friends. I wouldn't trade this minute for anything. Sneaking in girls' rooms, making out at parties, flirting and playing games, they had nothing on this moment. *Damn I'm sweet*, I thought.

"What?" Aspen asked, turning in my arms to look at me.

"What, what?"

"You chuckled."

I did? "Nothing. Just thinking about how cool I am." She rolled her eyes at me. "And how lucky."

She leaned up and kissed me. It went straight to my head, making me dizzy and sweaty, and yeah, I'll admit it, horny.

We sat out there for hours. Lame as it sounds, we made s'mores and told ghost stories. The girls tried to get a game of truth or dare out of us, but Jaden and I took a stand. There was only so much cheese we'd allow in one night. We talked, laughed, and the only time I didn't have Aspen in my arms was when I replaced her with my guitar. Apparently, I couldn't deny her anything. I played a few songs, more than I'd planned, but girls love music, and the way Aspen looked at me when I played? I'd play all night for that look. It was like she touched me, and I'll tell you, I definitely hungered for her touch.

Around midnight we doused the fire and headed back to the house. What a perfect night. My three best friends in the world were there, and even Pris and Jaden got along. As we got ready for bed, I knew it would only get better. She wore a pair of little flannel shorts and a tank top and I climbed into bed in nothing but my basketball shorts. I put my hand on my cheek, leaning on my elbow and looked down on her.

"This weekend has been perfect," she whispered. I felt her breath against my skin, and it made me shiver.

"Funny, I was just thinking the same thing about tonight."

She sighed. "I'm happy, Bastian."

The moonlight shined bright enough in the room that I could see her face. "You're beautiful," I told her and meant it more than anything.

"You just want to get some." She laughed.

"Damn it. You figured out my plan!" We both laughed. "Really though, it's not about that." I used my free hand to brush the side of her face with my fingers. "Okay, so it's kind of like I won the lottery, ya know? You're my best friend. Always have been and always will be, but now I can say you're my girl, too. I just want you to know . . ." I shrugged. What did I want her to know? I had no idea what I was saying. "That I know how lucky I am, and that I think you're pretty amazing."

"You're amazing, too." Her voice was all wobbly. *Shit.* The last thing I wanted to do is make her cry. Happy tears or not, girls crying freaked me out. I always felt like I should do something, but half the time never knew what to do.

"Well, we knew that." I smiled and then I kissed her. Her arms wrapped around my neck and did that hair thing that I now freakin' loved. My mouth pressed to hers harder, not rough, but wanting to get as close to her as possible. Rolling over, I rested on top of her, lost in the feel of her. Did I say it was like I won the lottery? Even that had nothing on the way she made me feel. Our mouths learned each other's, molding together, teasing and tasting. I let my hand ghost under her shirt, going slow so I didn't miss any signal if I needed to stop.

"It's okay," she whispered so I kept going. Brushing the bottom of her breast. I didn't go any farther. Of course, I would have if she'd told me she wanted to, but I was happy just letting my tongue twine with hers and to tease her soft skin.

When I pulled away, still letting my fingers play with her hair like they were the strings on my guitar, I talked to her until she fell asleep. It was so small, that it could feel like nothing to someone else, but to me, it was epic.

I slipped out of Aspen's arms and grabbed my vibrating cell phone. My mom's number flashed across the screen. Sneaking out of the room, I clicked the talk button, trying to sound as cool as I could. I definitely wasn't supposed to be sleeping with Aspen hours away from home right now.

174

"Morning, Ma."

"Hey, kiddo. Are you having fun with Jaden?"

My whole body tensed. She'd been crying. I knew that crack in her voice. The fake, syrupy sweetness that she tried to use to cover her pain. "What's wrong?" I asked, going out onto the porch.

"Nothing, honey. Just wanted to check on you."

My whole body still felt tight. "Ma, I know you better than that. What happened?" Funny how your heart could race the same way when you're excited as it did when you were scared.

"It's nothing you need to worry about, Bastian. It's just . . . Roger and I broke up. I didn't call to talk about that though. I wanted to check on you."

I'd kill him. My hand fisted my phone tightly. How could he go from wanting to propose to her to breaking her heart this quickly? It was always the same thing. "Are you okay?" This time it was my voice that cracked.

"Just tired." She sighed. "Tired of screwing up, of hurting. I just want to talk to my boy. You always have been, and always will be, the best thing in my life."

I squeezed my eyes shut. I didn't want her to hurt. I didn't want to hurt, but it always happened this way, didn't it? I fought tears. I couldn't let myself punk out like that. What did it ever help? So I talked to her, made her laugh the way I always did when she was upset, wondering what made her think this was worth it? Didn't she just say this time was different? And Roger, the asshole. He'd said he loved her. What a joke. And they'd made me fall for it, too. How was this worth it? Hook-ups were so much easier than this.

How did I know I wouldn't be like Roger, or my dad, or all the other guys in the past and just change my mind? I thought I loved Aspen, but what if I didn't? What if I kept this going and hurt her? I hated the crack in my mom's voice, the tears she tried to hide behind her words. I wanted to protect her and failed, but I wouldn't with Aspen. Even if I had to protect her from me. One weekend would be easier to get over than if we kept this going. My fists clenched as I felt a weight in my chest.

When I got off the phone, I woke everyone up and told them we had to leave. She kept touching me and trying to talk to me and even though my fingers still pricked from the feel of her skin beneath mine, I kept my distance.

My whole body hurt, a heavy ache pressing down on my chest the whole drive home. They'd all stopped asking what was wrong about halfway. I was sick to my stomach and deserved it. I deserved much more than that.

I followed Aspen through her empty house and up to her room when we got back home. I fought the urge to run, but I wasn't a coward. I'd man-up and do what was right.

"Is everything okay?" she asked, trying to pull me into a hug when we got into her room.

I looked down at her, and that sexy blush on my best friend's face. I almost told her no, the words begged to fall from my mouth, but I didn't. I was doing this for her. She trusted me and crazy as it sounded, this was my way of deserving that trust by giving us an out before we got in too deep, and it hurt even more when things unraveled. "Um, not really. Aspen, I . . ." *Come on, Hawkins. Do it.* "It's over."

CHAPTER THIRTEEN

Was it possible for words to singe your tongue? That's how it felt. Like it burned, and left a gross taste in my mouth. It wasn't over, except, I'd just made it that way, hadn't I? And I wouldn't take it back. I couldn't.

Aspen stepped away from me, and I crossed my arms so I wouldn't be tempted to pull her close again. "What do you mean?"

"Us." I shrugged. "This whole thing. I mean, not our friendship," I quickly tried to clarify. I couldn't lose her completely. "The other part though. It wouldn't work, so why prolong it?"

"Actually, I thought it was working pretty well!" Her voice was hard. I hated hearing it directed at me that way. "Sorry that our *weekend* together was too long for you!"

I squinted my eyes and rubbed my forehead. I hated this, but I had to do it. "This is coming out wrong. I just . . . the long term thing just never works, and if we keep going, then someone is going to get hurt." Couldn't she see I was doing the right thing?

Aspen poked my chest. "Too late for that. You promised me I wasn't like the rest of them, Sebastian, and I trusted you. The long term thing doesn't work, because you don't want it to!" She stepped farther away from me, hugging herself. I wanted to pull her closer to me. My arms should be comforting her, not her own, but I knew that would just make it worse.

"You're not like the rest of them, Woodstock. I—"

She cut me off. "Don't call me that."

I'm not going to lie, that hurt. I'd called her Woodstock since we were kids. I didn't get why she didn't understand that I just didn't want to hurt her in the long run. "I don't want things to be messed up. This relationship thing never goes the way it's supposed to. I'm trying to save us from dealing with that. Can't we just be us again? Aspen and Sebastian?"

"Things are screwed up because you made them that way. Because you're Sebastian freakin' Hawkins, and you can't settle down with one girl. I should have known you'd pull this shit." Her eyes started to water. Those tears were suffocating me. This is what I didn't want! Her hurting. My mom hurting. All of this was just fucked up.

"Come here." I reached out for her; that zap

happening when I touched her hand. I just wanted to make her feel better. I tried pulling her close, for herself just as much as me, but she jerked away. It was like a punch to the gut.

"No! You can't make this better. It's your fault."

Her pain collided with mine and erupted. "I'm trying to be noble here! Don't you get that?!"

Her tears flowed freely now. "Noble? You have a funny way of showing it. I was over you, and you made me think we had a chance, and now you're crushing me."

What did that even mean? This was the second time she said she'd been over me, but I knew she wasn't. Her words and my thoughts were all trying to push through at the same time. I was confused and hurt that she didn't understand. Angry at myself that I was hurting her, and angry at her, too. "Funny, Aspen, but I know you weren't over me considering I've been giving you advice for weeks on how to hook-up with me."

Her face paled, and I regretted the words immediately. I was totally screwing this up, and I didn't even know what to do about it. "Wood—"

"You're The Hook-up Doctor?" she stepped up to me and pushed me. Hard. I fell back onto her bed. "You jerk! You lied to me!"

"What? No I didn't. I didn't tell you, but I never lied." I stood up.

"So that's what this was all about. You never really wanted me. It was only because you thought I wanted you. Why take the easy hook-up for the weekend?! I hate you, Sebastian. Get out of my house!" She was crying, her face red, but not from blushing. It was so different, that red, when it came from hurt and anger than embarrassment.

"No. That's not it. It had nothing to do with the emails. They just made me realize I should go for it."

The tightness in her features, the way her eyes narrowed at me in hate told me I'd just said the wrong thing. "Well guess what, Mr. Hook-up Doctor. *You were wrong*. I wasn't trying to get with you. It was Matt! He's the one I wanted to go out with, not you!"

My chest started to hurt. My heart was pounding like a jackhammer against my ribs. Matt? *Matt?* That ass! "That doesn't make sense. You helped me when I told PA to be nice. You ditched us when I said to ignore him." My head was spinning. "At the party you were supposed to flirt. You saw me with Crystal and got nervous and got drunk."

"*God*. You're so conceited, Bastian. Matt was at the arcade. He was at the party, too. I know you may think it does, but the world doesn't revolve around

181

you! Looks like you don't know it all like you think you do! But thanks for helping me. I'm sure I can put all this to good use, when I tell Matt I like him."

Her words had an effect over my whole body. They weakened the muscles in my legs. I felt hot all over and not the good kind of hot either. But more than that, I felt like I'd seen my mom feel so many times. Broken. I had to get out of there. "You know what? You can have him. I couldn't care less. When you get your little boyfriend, don't forget my other fifty bucks."

She slammed her bedroom door when I walked out. Each step I took away from her made another pain shoot through my body, but I kept going. She didn't want me anyway, so I'd find a way not to want her either. I was The Hook-up Doctor, so I'd go out there and do what I did best. Hook-up. Jaden had been right all along. Girls were crazy.

"Ma, quit hogging all the Chunky Monkey." I grabbed the pint of ice cream off Mom's lap as she sat next to me on the couch. I wasn't proud of myself. Actually, I was pretty embarrassed that I was practically crying in my ice cream with my *mom*. Totally not a very manly thing to do, but I just couldn't make myself go out tonight. Everything about it felt wrong. Plus,

I didn't want to leave Mom alone tonight. She needed me, so I'd be there. I tried to tell myself that was the real reason I'd turned into a sap, eating ice cream and watching a bad romance movie after a break-up, but even I knew that wasn't true.

"Hey! This is supposed to be my "poor-me" night. That entitles me to more of the ice cream," she said. I tossed the pint back at her, because it was much easier to hand over the dessert rather than tell her I was in mourning, too. I saved some points on the "losing my masculinity" scale if no one knew what I was doing but me. "Speaking of, you don't have to stay home with me tonight, kiddo. I'm fine." She grabbed my hand, and I wanted to tell her I wasn't. I clamped my mouth closed when she continued. "We're fine."

"Yeah, we are." I finished the movie with her before heading up to bed. The next morning I was supposed to go back to work, but I couldn't do it. What if she'd gone to Matt after I left? I can't believe the jack-off was the one she'd wanted from the start. They were probably together by now, and I couldn't risk making pizza while they snuck in the back room to make out or something. That's what I'd planned on doing with her the first time we worked together after hooking up.

So, I faked a killer cough, something I'd done for

school a million times, and called in. Irresponsible and lame? Yeah, but I figured I deserved it. I thought about calling Jaden, but I couldn't do it. He wouldn't understand, and I wasn't in the mood to hear I told you so, or him to go all Mike Tyson on me because, even though he's the one who told me girls were crazy, this would still end up my fault. So I got dressed, grabbed my skateboard and went for a ride to clear my head.

Even the jumps at the skate park didn't help. Sure, that little rush of adrenaline, the jump of my heart when I landed felt good, but not good enough to make me forget that when I walked away last night, Aspen had been crying, and that I was the one who put those tears on her face. And the guy I hated was probably wiping those tears away for her. Yeah, before I just had a bad feeling about him, but now I hated him. Funny how quickly that could happen.

Slipping my board under my arm I walked away from the skate ramps and over to the grassy area of the park. I wandered down one of the paths that led to the small creek. We had some prime entertainment in this town. I plopped down under a tree.

"Hi. You're Sebastian, right?"

I looked behind me.

It was Party Girl. Twin party girl without her other

half. She had on a sinfully short pair of shorts and a tank top that I'm embarrassed to say, I couldn't even be happy about. "What's up? Crystal, right?" She sat down next to me, and I fought a groan. Hadn't I just said I needed to get back to my roots? Right now, I just wasn't feelin' it, but I didn't want to be a jerk, either.

"Yep. I borrowed my cousin's car while she's at work, so I was out trying to find something to do." She pushed her black hair behind her ear and looked at me.

"Good luck with that. We're pretty scarce on the fun around here."

"Ya think?" She smiled at me. I couldn't help but laugh. "So what are you doing out here by yourself? Where are your friends? Or the girl. How'd things go with her?"

What was it with girls and talking? Even the ones I didn't know acted like it was share your feelings hour all the time. "Ugh . . ." I grunted, hoping she'd get a clue. No such luck.

"Uh-oh. What did you do?" she asked.

I whipped my head around, more than a little annoyed. "What the hell? Why does it automatically have to be *me* who did something wrong?"

She shrugged. "Because you're the guy."

185

Okay, so Jaden was scoring even more points to prove his whole girls are crazy theory. "What kind of wacko knowledge is that? I swear, no wonder girls need my help. They're all freakin' mental." I was done with girls. Aspen, Pris, Crystal, I didn't want anything to do with any of them. How did I ever think I knew what they wanted? They were even more messed up than guys were! Well, except for my mom. She just had radar for assholes, but all the rest of the girls I knew, they needed way more than a little bit of help from The Hook-up Doctor.

I pushed to my feet, but Crystal grabbed my hand to stop me. I jerked it away because it felt weird; some other girl holding onto me like that.

"I'm kidding. You know, angry ex-girlfriend here, remember? I have girl-power music playing in the car if you need more proof."

I sat back down. It wasn't like I had anywhere else to go. I was avoiding all my friends. I scratched my head, hoping my arms would block her view of me. "Come to find out, she really liked someone else." I couldn't believe I told her that.

She pulled her knees to her chest the way Aspen sat sometimes. "Yeah, Will, too. I guess that was the real reason he broke up with me. It's always someone else."

Of course, I'd neglected to tell her I'd dumped Aspen, and that's how I found out about the other guy, but what did that matter if I hadn't been the one she wanted, anyway? "This is kind of a first for me," I admitted. "I'm not trying to sound cocky, but I mean, I've never really given it a chance for there to be someone else, ya know? I knew how things always play out though. I don't know why I even went there."

"Because you loved her. That's why I gave Will a chance even though everyone told me he was a player."

"Arrgh." I rubbed a hand over my face. "I really don't want to talk about this. It's a guy thing. We can do serious for maybe ninety seconds before we shut down." She laughed like I hoped she would. "I mean, I'm sorry about your ex, but I'm sure you don't want to talk about him anymore than I want to talk about Aspen." And Matt . . . Who was probably kissing her right now . . . I needed to distract myself.

"I was thinking about going to the mall. Want to come?"

"Sure." I stood and helped her up, too. It felt kind of good to hang out with someone who knew what I was going through. Plus, even though I knew what I really needed was to get back on the saddle so to speak, I totally didn't feel like it. At least with her, I

187

knew she still had feelings for her ex. Made things easier when I didn't have to worry about her getting the wrong idea.

A couple of hours later we were sitting at a table in the food court, eating food worse than what we served at DJ's, when my blood went cold.

She was here.

With him.

Son of a—

"Sebastian? What's wrong?"

"Shh." I shushed Crystal like her words blocked my vision or something. They were quite a ways down the walkway, looking over the edge toward the bottom floor, but I could recognize her body anywhere. I knew it now. Every curve, how her hair fell, and what it felt like when the hand she had wrapped around Mattie's had held mine.

My insides were frozen. Like one little flick from her finger and they would break apart like an icicle hitting the ground. I'd never felt anything like it, and honestly, I never wanted to again. How could my mom have thought love was worth it if it had the power to make you feel like this?

"Is that her? With him?" Crystal must have turned around to see what I was looking at, but I couldn't pull my eyes off Aspen long enough to see. I couldn't believe it! Last night she was crying over me, and now, here she was holding some other guy's hand at the mall? I squinted so I could see better. Had she dropped his hand? Yep, she did. She pulled free, and now she was walking away. Oh, and the jerk was following her.

"Come on," I told Crystal as I started walking away, fully aware that I was teetering on stalker territory as I followed her.

I heard her scramble behind me. "What are we doing?" she asked. Hell if I knew, but I kept walking anyway. And that's when it happened. She stopped, and turned around. Our eyes locked, her green gaze grabbing me. I had the urge to punch Mattie and kiss her at the same time. I didn't know which was stronger. They weren't holding hands still, but that didn't matter. I knew what he was thinking. I'd been *him* for so long that I knew he wasn't serious about her.

But I didn't do either. No kissing, no punching. I don't know what made me do it. Maybe I wanted her to hurt like I was. Maybe I'd gone as mental as the female population seemed to be, but even as I did it, I knew it was a mistake. My hand jerked over, and I grabbed Crystal's, linking our fingers together in a clear message: Aspen had moved on, and so had I.

Even though I hadn't, but that was beside the point.

Right now, I just needed something to do, and this was the only thing I could think of. I had to give Crystal props, because she didn't pull away. Her hand was tense, and I heard her breath hitch, but she didn't drop my hand.

"What's up?" I asked, hoping my voice came out steadier than I felt.

Aspen didn't reply. Her mouth was opened in a small "O", her eyes matching it. I wanted to walk over to her, brush my hand across her face like I'd done this weekend, until she smiled instead of looking . . . hurt? Yes, that's what she looked like, and I realized that wasn't what I wanted. Even though I was hurting, I didn't want her to feel the same.

"You don't look sick to me," Mattie said.

"Huh?" *Shit*. I wondered if he would rat me out to the boss. "No one asked you."

My words seemed to snap Aspen out of her shock. "Who's your date?" Her words were clipped.

"Who's yours?" I asked, immediately wanting the words back. *Who's yours?* Like I didn't know who this guy was. This whole situation was really messing with my skills. "This is Crystal." I tried to cover up my idiotic screw up by tossing Crystal's name at them.

"I know you," Matt started. "I saw you guys talking at the party."

It was official. Before all this was over, I'd definitely be punching Mattie in the nose. His smirk told me he knew exactly what he'd just done. I groaned.

"Oh, I see how it is. So, I was the backup girl this weekend? Crystal at the party, me at the beach house, and now you're back to her? God, I hate you, Sebastian!" Aspen's arms were crossed over her chest, something dark twisting the green of her eyes. Yeah, she was pissed, but so was I.

"What about you? You're the one kissing me when you wanted this punk." I pointed to Mattie.

"Dude, watch what you call me," Mattie replied, and I stepped toward him.

"Or what? What are you going to do about it, Mattie?" Yeah, I used the name he hated. So sue me.

"Sebastian, maybe we should go." Crystal grabbed my arm, which made Aspen react.

"Maybe you should go. No one wants *you* here, anyway," Aspen told her.

Crystal snapped back. "Listen, I'm not taking sides here. I'm just trying to defuse the situation."

"Oh, aren't you just the sweet, little girlfriend. Watch your back. He never sticks around for long."

"Hey!" I replied to Aspen. "No one said she's my girlfriend, and why do you care if I stick around? You had this loser in the wings the whole time!"

"Dude, I said to watch what you say to me," the idiot said.

Aspen started in on Crystal again, while I told Mattie where he could stick it. It was stupid, and loud, but I didn't care. I had enough with this guy, and I wanted to make sure he knew it. But, at the same time, I didn't really want Crystal and Aspen to get into it either. People were circling around us, enjoying the show; and all I wanted was this jerk away from Aspen.

"You better not be playing games with her," I told him, but it was Aspen who answered me.

"*Him?* You're the one who plays games." Her hands were balled into fists, but her eyes, the white was tinted red, like she was crying.

"I don't trust him, Woodstock." He'd hurt her. I mean, I know I had hurt her; but I actually loved her, too. That put me a little lower on the asshole scale than he was.

"You don't have to." She turned to Mattie. "Come on, Matt. Let's go." She grabbed his hand as they walked away, and it took everything in me not to tackle the guy from behind, but instead I pulled my bonehead number whatever move.

"Aspen! He doesn't deserve you! I know what I'm talking about! You came to me for help, remember?

I know this shit!" I was yelling. Through the mall. See what love does to you?

A hand clamped on my shoulder. "Sir, we're going to have to ask you to come with us."

Oh, shit.

CHAPTER FOURTEEN

Getting kicked out of the mall was not one of my finer moments. Dinged my ego a bit more when they had to call my mom. Something about me being a minor. Whatever.

"You're going to have to explain this to me, Sebastian. I get called out of work because you were screaming in the middle of the mall? What's gotten into you?" my mom asked, crossing her arms in pissed-off-mom mode while we stood by her car in the parking lot.

Love. Girls. Insanity. I had quite a few words I could throw at Mom about what had gotten into me, but I settled on trying to smooth things over. "It's not that big a deal, Ma. You know how mall cops are. He just wanted to flex his muscles."

Her eyes narrowed, and I'm not afraid to admit it, my heart rate kicked up. This was beyond mad, into irate territory.

"This isn't a joke! I had to cancel a class to come and get you. They said you were yelling at a girl? I raised you better than that, Sebastian."

Yeah, she had. If there was one thing she always told me it was to respect girls, and what had I done? Yelled at Aspen. My best friend. In the middle of the mall. How had things gotten so royally messed up? But it wasn't my fault. I'd been trying to do exactly what my mom taught me to do, and that was to not hurt a girl. "I know. I'm sorry. It was a misunderstanding."

"It was my fault. I started it." I looked over my shoulder at Crystal who had been giving us some space. "I was having a bad day and took it out on Sebastian. I didn't mean to get us in any trouble."

I closed my mouth so the shock wouldn't show. This girl was totally saving my butt. "See, Ma? We've made up." I looked at Crystal. "But it wasn't your fault. I'm sure I deserve some of the credit for this." I put my arm around her so it would look like we'd been the ones fighting, and now we were all peachy. Mom sighed.

"I don't like this, but I have to get back to work. I don't want something like this happening again, Sebastian." She looked at Crystal, then me, then Crystal.

Oh! "So, sorry for yelling at you." I kicked at the ground. I hated apologizing for stuff I *did*. Saying sorry for something I didn't do sucked even worse.

"No harm, no foul," she replied.

"Come on. I need to drop you off at home before I go back into work," Mom told me. Crystal piped up next and offered a ride, which my mom reluctantly agreed to after telling me she wanted me not to leave the house for the rest of the day.

When we were locked away in Crystal's car, I turned to thank her, but she cut me off. "Don't even think about saying thank you. What the hell did you pull in there?"

Oops. Looked like I traded in pissed off mom for another angry girl. "I don't know! It was a reflex."

"It was a pretty stupid one! I mean, I get you not trusting that guy since he was definitely calling my cousin this weekend to try and get in her pants." My whole body froze up. I knew I didn't trust that guy! Why did I break up with her just so some other guy could play games with her? I'd meant to save her pain, not make her prey for someone else. "I guess it could be different with them. It's obvious she likes him." It was obvious she liked him? I didn't see that. Or maybe I just didn't *want* to see it. She was supposed to like me, not that jerk.

Oblivious to my mixed-up thoughts, Crystal kept talking, "None of that really matters though. Do you not know girls at all?"

With that one little question, a light bulb went off

in my head. I *did* know girls. When it came to the opposite sex, I knew how to get what I wanted. I was The Hook-up Doctor, right? And yeah, I know I'd just broken up with her, but I did it for her own good, and Mattie wouldn't play by those rules. He'd hurt her, so really, if I put a plan in action to get her back, I'd be doing it for her own good. But then, what about the rest of it? I'd gotten more proof love didn't work since Mom's ex-putz broke up with her, but really this was more about saving Aspen than my love for her. Okay, so I was probably a little delusional with that one, because the pain in my chest when I saw her with him devastated me, but saving her from Mattie playing her was worth it.

Plus, I hated losing. I couldn't stand the thought of him with her, not just because I loved her, but because I hated him. Did that make me a jerk? Probably, but there wasn't much I could do about that. This was it. I was doing this for Aspen's own good. "Hey. I need you to be my girlfriend."

"What?!" Crystal jerked her car to the side of the road.

"Well, not really, but I want you to pretend to be with me. I need your help to win Aspen back."

Crystal looked skeptical, shaking her head. "Not so sure that's the right way to go about this, Sebastian."

I laughed. If anyone knew how to get the girl, it was me. I wasn't going to let Matt do to her what I was trying to save her from. "Trust me. I know what I'm doing."

My hands were shaking. *Shaking*. Like I'd never gone out with a girl before. Of course, I wasn't really going out with this one, but it would look like it after tonight. It felt wrong, a heavy weight embedded itself in the pit of my stomach, and I couldn't get rid of it no matter what I did. I didn't understand it. This should be a piece of cake. All I had to do was pretend I was over her. Play the whole nonchalance game I'd told so many girls to play in the past. Make it look like I'd moved on, so she would want me more. Hopefully, in the meantime, I could get something on Mattie, some kind of proof that he was an asshole before he had the chance to prove it by hurting Aspen. I doubted she would believe me if I told her Crystal said he tried to land her cousin.

Then I could swoop in and get the girl. I had no idea what I'd do with her once I had her, because I still didn't trust the whole love thing.

It was all so easy. It *should* be easy, but instead it felt . . . wrong. Not the whole getting Mattie out of the picture thing or even the getting the girl thing, because I did still love her. I think, if anything, seeing her with him made me realize I loved her even more than I thought I had; but something felt off, and I couldn't put my finger on what it was.

This had been the only time I liked the gossip of a small town. I heard through the grapevine that Pris and Aspen were going to be at the arcade tonight. All it took was one phone call to Jaden, and he was game to go out. Crystal took a little more persuasion, but in the end, she agreed. I stood out front of my house waiting for her in a pair of blue jeans, black t-shirt and a blue button up shirt over it, left open.

I mumbled a "hi" to her when I got in the car, my stomach feeling like I imagined Aspen's did the night she spewed all over my ex-lucky shirt. Aside from the directions I gave her, we were quiet the whole way there.

"Are you sure you want to do this?" she asked after we parked. "If you are serious about her, you should just talk to her. I can't tell you how much I wish Will would tell me he loved me."

"Yeah," I said quickly. "This will work." *It has to work.* She shook her head as she opened the car door, but I stopped her. "You're pretty cool for helping me out, Crystal. I appreciate it, and if it counts for anything, I think Will is a dumbass."

I let go of her, and we both got out of the car. It would look more real if I held her hand, but I couldn't bring myself to do it. In the mall it had been an automatic reaction. I hadn't really thought about it, and now that I could—it might be weird—but it made me feel like I was cheating or something. I browsed the room with my eyes, not seeing Pris and Aspen, or Jaden who was supposed to meet me here. He was always late. We sat down next to each other in a booth.

"Did you tell your friend what's going on with me?" Crystal asked.

I shook my head. "Nah. I haven't even told him about Aspen, yet. It's not a big deal. I can explain it to him when he gets here."

We sat there for a few more minutes, neither of us saying a word. My eyes were still searching out Aspen, my attention drawn to Crystal when she excused herself to go to the bathroom. As soon as she was gone, someone plopped down across from me. I expected it to be Jaden, but it was Paul, this other guy we went to school with. "Who's the hottie?" he asked.

Hottie? "Huh?"

"Um, the girl you're sitting here with? She's freaking gorgeous."

It's funny because I didn't even notice. I mean, I knew she was pretty, but I was so distracted tonight, thinking about Aspen and wondering if Mattie would be with her, that I didn't notice anything else. I felt a little stab of guilt. I'm sure she didn't care if I noticed her that way. She still had feelings for her ex, and she obviously knew I was wrapped up in Aspen, but I felt like a jerk, because she *was* helping me. What if she did start getting the wrong idea? Holy crap, what if there was more to the reason she'd agreed to this? I didn't think so, but couldn't be for sure. "She's a friend," I mumbled. Paul said something about me being lucky before leaving, and Crystal sat back down.

"You look nice," I told her, feeling obligated. I mean, she did look pretty, but again, it felt like I wasn't being sincere, because it wasn't Aspen I was saying this to.

"Um . . . thanks?"

"I know I already thanked you, but I want to be sure you know I really do appreciate your help. And . . ." I felt like an idiot. "And Aspen, I do love her. I just didn't want you to get—"

Her hysterical laughter cut me off.

"What's so funny?" I was slightly annoyed.

Crystal held up her hand. "Believe me. You don't have to do this, Sebastian. I'm not getting the wrong idea here. I'm really just trying to help. You're cool, but I don't see you like that."

"Oh. Well, good." *I'm a jackass.*

"Am I interrupting?" Jaden stood at the end of the table, his arms crossed over his chest, his jaw locked.

"Nah, just wondering where you were," I said waiting for him to sit down, but he didn't. What was his problem? I looked over at Crystal and it clicked. "This is Crystal, not Abby."

If anything my words seemed to make him madder. "She's also not Aspen."

"Hey. Chill out." I got that he was a little confused, since I'd been feeling too sorry for myself to tell him everything that went down lately, but it also wasn't fair to take it out on Crystal. "It's not what you think, Jay."

"Dude, you even said yourself Aspen and Pris were different. I thought, for sure, you weren't stupid enough to blow her off."

Now that pissed me off. "Me, stupid? Look at you! You've been doing this little dance around Pris forever. Why don't you grow a pair and go for her instead of hanging out with me so I can get you girls?" Jaden's face paled, and I immediately regretted my words. This was my boy. We always had each other's back, and what I'd just said to him was messed up. "Dude, just let me explain. We're not really—"

"I hung out with you because you were my friend, not for girls. I can get those on my own, and apparently, you can, too. So many you don't know how to handle them all." Jaden put his hands flat on the table and leaned toward me. "As for Pris? Not all of us can live in your fantasy Sebastian-land where we all get what we want. I may not have gone for her, but that's because I knew I would screw it up. Just like you thought you had it under control, but all you did was mess it up. I'm done. You're lucky you're my boy because you have no idea how much I want to knock you out right now." Jaden turned to leave.

It took me a minute to find my tongue. I was in shock, confused and a little pissed off. Not thinking, I stood. "Did you ever think she didn't want me? Why does it have to be my fault?" I fell back into the seat, holding my head with both hands. What was going on here? Why had Jaden just freaked out on me without giving me a chance to explain?

"Sebastian, are you sure you know what you're doing?"

No. "Yeah. It's under control. I just have to explain to Jaden what's going on, and he'll understand. He's probably just mad because I didn't tell him." I added that on the heaping pile of things that didn't feel right. There was more to what Jaden said than I understood, but it wasn't my fault. He was the one being all secretive and angry. It's not like he wasn't just as bad as me when it came to girls and this thing with Crystal wasn't even real. "We're sticking to the plan."

I leaned back in the booth, my whole body wracked with tension. Crystal was quiet while I sat there with my eyes closed trying to figure everything out. I don't know what made me open them when I did, but as they popped open, I saw Aspen. She looked at Pris and smiled; man, I wished she was smiling at me like that. This weekend, when she'd looked at me, it felt like I was the king of the world, now when I pictured her, I only saw the look on her face when I told her it was over.

The anger in her eyes when she admitted she really wanted Mattie. I didn't get it—why or how I'd somehow hurt her when she knew she was about to rip my heart out, but that smile—it almost made me forget it all. Everything inside me told me to stand up and go talk to her. That rush of adrenaline was back. Leaning over to Crystal, I started, "I'll be." The 'right back' died in my throat when Mattie walked up beside Aspen.

He put his hand on the small of her back, and I tensed. I could have sworn she did at the same time. Was he touching her when she didn't want to be touched? Aspen smiled again, but this one not as big as she put an arm around Pris. The movement pulled her away from Mattie, but then she crooked her finger for him to follow them.

"I'm sorry . . ." Crystal fidgeted in her seat.

"No biggie." But it was. We both knew it. How did everything get so screwed up?

I watched them as they sat at a table. It was kind of perfect, like the crowds of people parted so I had them in perfect view. Pris and Aspen were talking all animated like they always did, their hands moving just as fast as their mouths. Mattie looked a little out of the loop, sitting across the table, but me, I just liked watching them. Sure, I was pretty much crossing the line between crush and creepy stalker, but no one knew that. Well, except Crystal.

I snickered when Aspen made a weird face, scrunching up her eyes and frowning when Mattie said something. Yeah, she didn't like whatever he said. I could tell. So, I know this made me sound like a sap, but as I kept my eyes trained on them, watching that happiness and excitement, the heaviness in my chest eased up. I didn't feel so weighed down. Crazy the power girls had over us, and they didn't even know it.

Leaning back in my seat, I slid my arm behind Crystal on the top of the seat. I wasn't touching her, just stretching as I made myself comfortable, and it was at that exact moment that her eyes wandered to me. My arm jerked, like it automatically wanted to pull away, but I fought to keep it there. Suddenly, the idea of making her jealous made my gut churn, but I'd already started. Might as well see it through, right?

But she just looked away and finished her conversation.

No pause, no eyes looking at me like she wanted me the way I wanted her. Nothing. Ice pricked across my skin, making me uncomfortable. "I gotta go." I was done. I couldn't spend the whole night watching her with Mattie, sitting here with Crystal, when I really wanted to be with Aspen.

Once more, I glanced at their table, only to see one less person there that should be.

"Outside. Now, Bastian." I froze at the sound of Pris's voice. She was pissed, and a pissed off Pris scared even me.

Shaking my head, I followed her retreating figure with Crystal right behind me. My life was a mess. I lost my girl, and now I was about to get my ass kicked by another one. Great.

As soon as we stepped into the hot, black night Pris turned on me. "What the hell, Sebastian? You said she was different. You said you loved her. I should kick your ass right now. What were you thinking?! How could you have done this to her?" Her black hair was curly and swinging as she spoke erratically to me.

I rubbed my head, a little irritated she was acting like this was all *my* fault. I wasn't the one who contacted me to hook-up with Mattie. I wasn't the one sitting in there with him right now. Well, that's because Crystal was with me, but that was different. "Um, I'm not really sure which one of those questions you expect me to answer first."

Wrong. Thing. To. Say. I dodged her fist that flew at me. "What the hell, Pris?"

"You stupid jerk! Do you have any brains in that head of yours? Idiot." She swung again, her words as wild as her fists. "Loser. *Es stupido.*"

"Stop." I caught her hand. "Why is everyone so mad at me? She's the one who moved on to Mattie in like two seconds."

"What? Did you expect her to hang around and wait for you? You're the one who dumped her, Bastian.

One day you told her she was different and the next you kicked her to the curb. And I thought *you* were different." Pris huffed and walked away, her last words hitting me in the chest. I was different. I didn't go around playing girls. They all knew I didn't do the relationship thing from the beginning, and with Aspen, I thought I would. That didn't make me like them, did it? The kind of guys who broke my mom's heart all those times.

"You dumped her?"

I rolled my eyes. Here we went again.

"Why does it matter, Crystal? I told you she wanted someone else, anyway."

She had that same look in her eyes Jaden had. The one Pris had. Disappointment.

"It matters, Sebastian. I never would have done this with you if I would have known you're the one who broke her heart. I have to go." She frowned like I'd let her down.

For the third time in one night, someone I considered a friend turned their back on me and walked away. "She didn't want me! She was trying to get him the whole time! Why don't you guys understand that?" I yelled at her, but she didn't turn around. I leaned against the wall, elbows on my knees and my head

in my hand. For the first time in my life, I was alone.
This answered the question I'd asked Mom. No, love
wasn't worth it. And now it was pretty clear, I definitely
didn't know what I was doing.

CHAPTER FIFTEEN

I looked around my bedroom. It was official. I was depressed. Weird, considering I'd never dealt with it before. I had a pretty good life. Sure, I got upset about the crap with my mom, wondered about my dad and all that stuff like every other teenager, but I'd always been happy. I had my friends who I could always count on and girls when I wanted them. My pride was a big one. Knowledge because I'd been pretty sure I knew everything. Now . . . I wasn't so sure. All these dinged my pride. I was confused as hell, and I missed my friends.

Jaden, who I wanted to pop upside the head half the time, but who was always down for anything; and when push came to shove, he was really like a brother to me. He was much more than just a friend. I hated having him mad at me.

Pris, with her attitude and sharp tongue, but who I would do anything for. And Aspen. Man, I missed her. Not just the kissing and touching that I'd gotten pretty hooked on last weekend, but *her*. Her tornado of smiles, snark, and sweetness.

I was no longer whipped, I'd turned into a sappy punk, because all this had me so emo I feared someone might need to step in with an intervention.

Except there was no one to step in, because I'd pissed them all off.

Bored, I pulled my laptop off my bed and into my lap. Knowing there wouldn't be anything there—well at least not from the person I wanted to contact me—I logged into my Hook-up Doctor account. My pulse spiked when it said I had one new message, but plummeted just as quickly when I realized it wasn't from PA Rocks. What did that name mean anyway? I let myself wonder why she picked it while clicking on the new email. It was probably a new client, but I couldn't even find it in myself to care. What was the point?

Without viewing the message I closed down my email when I heard a soft rapping on my door. "Yeah." It had to be Mom, because she was the only person still talking to me. "Hey, Ma," I said to her as she slipped inside.

"Hey, kiddo. How ya doing?" She sat on my bed next to me. I shrugged, wondering how she knew anything was wrong. I definitely hadn't told her. "You seem down. Is everything okay with you? I haven't seen the gang around lately."

I groaned, really annoyed with the whole mom sixth sense thing. Of course, I'd hardly left my house for two days, which had to tell her something. Oh, and did I mentioned I lost my job, too? Well, I guess lost isn't the right word since I'd just stopped showing up. "Its fine, Ma. Everyone's just busy." I stood up and slipped my shoes on. I *so* wasn't in the mood to do this. "I think I'm going to go for a ride." Picking up my skateboard, I headed for my bedroom door.

"Bastian?" she called after me.

"Yeah."

"You know you can talk to me, right?" Mom was still sitting on my bed, looking like she hoped I would come back. But I didn't. Part of me wanted to, but I couldn't. I ran a hand through my hair, talking to her as I walked out.

"Nothing to talk about, Ma. I'll see you soon." With that I was gone.

I ended up back at the park. It was one of the only places close enough for me to walk or ride to. I took a few trips around, jumped a few ramps, but being as I had turned into Mr. Emo, I decided to sulk around the park instead. By now, I knew I'd screwed up. I'd pretty much taken ownership of the shit I was in, but there was that part of me, too, that felt betrayed. They'd all turned their backs on me, like it was all my fault. I couldn't understand why Jaden, Pris and Aspen had to make such a big deal out of all of this.

Weaving my way through the park, my feet rooted to the ground like the trees beside me when I saw *them*. Aspen and Mattie. Then, like the stalker I was becoming, I ducked behind one of those trees, putting my Bond skills to use.

A buzzing zapped through my body, echoing in my ears and pushing the blood through my veins with the force of a river's rapids. Man she was gorgeous, wearing a pair of blue jeans that hugged her body, a pink shirt and her hair in a simple pony tail that I used to want to pull just to annoy her. Now, I wanted to run my fingers through it because the soft strands felt so much better when I buried my hand in them, rather than trying to make her mad.

I was still mad at her, but it felt different when I could see her than when I couldn't. Watching her took some of that anger away. *God, I am lame.*

She shook her head at Mattie, crossing her arms over her chest. Oh, I knew that look! Her eyes were squinty, her body straight. "Ha, ha, Mattie. How does it feel to have her mad at you?" I whispered.

This time he shook his head as he said something

213

to her. I couldn't hear them, but knew I needed to say a prayer for my awesome eyesight, because I could see them so well. Aspen's arms flew in the air like she was at a loss as she said something. Mattie replied, and she definitely didn't like it. I felt butterflies—yeah, I said it—butterflies in my stomach; half of me happy they were fighting, but the other half, the one that kept pushing over and covering up the happy part, felt guilty. I hated the guy, but if she liked him, well, I didn't want her to hurt, either. Better me than her, right? At least until I found the proof that he was a douche.

Mattie reached out for her. Something inside me flared when she backed away. If she didn't want to be touched, the jerk better keep his hands off her. He stepped closer, and she took a step back, giving her head another shake. As I walked around the tree, no longer willing to hide in the corner in case she needed me, Mattie did us both a favor and walked away.

The opposite direction.

Score.

Because I had to see how she was doing. Her shoulders were hunched over and she looked . . . defeated. I hated seeing her that way. It killed me that *he* could cause her pain. That had to mean she really cared about him, right?

Taking a deep breath, I pushed those feelings aside, and trudged over to her. "Woodstock?"

Her head snapped up, tree-green eyes meeting mine. We held each other there, our sight grasping one another as tightly as my arms held her last weekend. It was in that moment, with all that pain swirling around in her eyes, the feel of her gaze as it wrapped around me, that I wanted to tell her. It didn't matter that we wouldn't last. That love always fell apart, and someone got hurt. I didn't care that she had feelings for Mattie, because I loved her, and that was supposed to be enough, right? You hear that all the time: love conquers all, but I'd never seen it, so I kept my mouth shut.

If she looked like that because of Mattie, then how I felt about her didn't matter. But making her feel better still did. "Are you okay? Need me to mess someone up for you? You know, my ninja skills and all." I tried for a joke, hoping that a flash of who we'd been would help us get there again.

If anything, it made things worse. The pain on her face multiplied, and if I saw what I thought I did, a flash of anger sparked, too. "Ha. I doubt you could kick the butt of the person who made me feel like this."

That little dent in my pride smashed in completely

215

and it shattered. Not only did she like Mattie, she thought I couldn't take him? "Whatever. I was just trying to help. I should beat his ass just to prove a point though."

"I'd like to see you try that one," she snapped back. Her eyes started getting watery, and I was trapped between telling her off for taking his side and trying to kiss those tears away.

"I'm just trying to help. I can see I'm not needed though." I leaned against a tree, trying to look like I didn't really care. "Lover's fight?" Her chin started to shake, and I felt that vibration inside me. I stepped toward her, ready to throw all my anger out the window if it made her feel better. It was like a need I felt inside me, pushing me to do whatever I could for her. "Baby, don't—"

She held up her hand, cutting off my "cry". "Don't call me that. I don't think your little girlfriend would appreciate it. Don't try to be smooth with me. You forget, I know your tricks. You're The Hook-up Doctor. You know all the best lines. All the right games to play, don't you? I'm done. You can take all your skills, Mr. Know-It-All and use them on someone else!"

Her tears were falling faster. Each and every drop, every word hitting me like the punch in the gut I deserved. Aspen's chest heaved in and out, while mine felt like it caved in. "I'm sorry." My voice cracked, and this time, it was me who walked away. I wasn't Mr. Know-It-All. I obviously didn't know jack, and it was time to ask for help.

I slammed my front door behind me, running into the bright living room. Mom sat on our beige couch, watching some soap opera or something on TV. I was too upset to even give her a hard time about it. "Ma!" I huffed, breathing like I'd run a marathon, which I practically had.

She jumped to her feet, worry creasing her brow. "What's wrong?"

I could hardly catch my breath enough to talk, but I knew I had to get this out. "I screwed up. Everything's so messed up, and I don't know what to do."

She pulled me to her, burying my face in her neck and stroking my hair. The light "shhh" whispering from her mouth like only a mom can do. Now, if anyone ever asked me, I would not admit to this moment. How much I needed my mom and trusted her, even though I had a feeling, when it came to love, she was just as confused as I was. But we always had each other. It was always her and me, and I trusted her.

"What's wrong, kiddo?"

With that, I pulled away from her. Yeah, I needed her, but I wasn't going to cry. I'd never let myself live that one down, and if she kept up with that "stroke and shush" thing, that's exactly what would have happened. Looking at my mom, I uttered the words I never thought I'd say to her. The words I dreaded hearing her say about another guy. "Ma, I'm in love."

This big, goofy smile spread across her face. "Aspen?" she asked, surprising me with her knowledge, but then I remembered she knew everything. Half the time I thought I was getting away with stuff, I wasn't. That was just Mom. We worked like that. She could read me, and I could read her. I was pretty lucky to have her.

"Aspen," I confirmed. If it was possible, her smile grew. "You're probably not going to be smiling when I tell you what happened."

"Oh, Bastian. What did you do?"

I walked over and fell onto the couch. "I think the better question is what didn't I do? You might want to sit down for this."

CHAPTER SIXTEEN

So, I spit it all out for her. Mom sat beside me quietly as I gave her the whole story. How I'd been getting money for hooking people up. That I started realizing I had feelings for Aspen, to finding out she was actually PA and deciding to go for it. While I was being honest, I even told her the truth about the weekend. There had been some serious head shakage going on when I admitted to going to the coast with Aspen, Pris and Jaden, but she still didn't speak up until I finished.

Mom did smile when I told her I really loved Aspen. That, cheesy as it sounded, I'd been the happiest I ever remembered being when we spent the weekend together. Of course, I took a few liberties and kept the whole bed sharing and making out on the beach that night a secret. Mom definitely didn't need details like that, and if I did come out of this with Aspen on my side, I'm sure she'd be pretty embarrassed if Mom knew.

After that, my gut clinched as I told her I broke up

with her. How I thought she was better off without me, because love always left people broken-hearted anyway. My stomach felt like I would hurl when I admitted to being jealous over Mattie and using Crystal to make her jealous. "So they all pretty much hope I die a fiery death. They want nothing to do with me." I fell back against the couch waiting for her to hand it to me, too.

Silence.

I started to feel a little itchy waiting for her to talk. The quiet rubbed me the wrong way. Yelling I could deal with, but I didn't want her to be disappointed in me. "Say something, Ma."

When she let out a breath, it was shaky. I knew that sound. It was more than disappointment. She was hurt. "I've really messed things up for us, haven't I, Bastian?"

My body lurched forward so I was sitting up again. "What? No. Believe me. This is anything but your fault. I did all of this myself." When the words came out of my mouth, I knew they were true. I'd tried to push some of the blame on Mattie, Aspen, Jaden and anyone else I could, but it had really been me.

"Tell me then. Why did you break up with Aspen? If the weekend was so great, why did you call it off?"

"Umm." I knew the answer to her question, but I had a feeling she did, too.

"Did you make that decision when I told you about Roger?" she asked. I hated doing it, but nodded my head.

Mom grabbed my hand. "I haven't been the best role model for you. I've made a lot of mistakes in my life, especially where men are concerned, but you know they are my mistakes, they don't have anything to do with you, Sebastian. I have no way of knowing what the future will hold for you and Aspen. You're both young and things happen, but because I've been hurt and made bad choices, that doesn't mean you'll hurt or be hurt. And if you are, that doesn't mean the same thing will happen with someone else."

I tried to slip my hand away from her, but she held it tight. "I'm serious. That's life. We win some, we lose some, but you can't live your life afraid of making my mistakes."

"You make it sound like it's been your fault!" I couldn't hold myself back from raising my voice. "All you did was love them, and they left you. I didn't want to do that with Aspen. Not after she got her feelings involved. Wasn't it better to cut our losses after two days, than for me to walk out on her like Dad walked out on you?" I blinked, hoping the move-ment would hold in the wetness pooling in my eyes. I didn't want to cry. Made me feel weak.

"Oh, Bastian." She rubbed a hand down the side of my face. "Always so noble. I'm so lucky to have a son who loves his mom so much, but as much as I wish it were true, I'm not perfect. I made just as many mistakes as your father. As Bill and John. Hell, I made more mistakes than Roger did. But again, those were my mistakes, and you kiddo, you're too good to really hurt someone. Your heart's always in the right place, even if you do make some mistakes."

I turned my head away from her, trying to wipe the stray tears away that managed to break free without her noticing. She grabbed my face and turned my head so I looked at her. "More importantly, you are not your dad. You're just Sebastian. My funny, smart, talented, *loyal, big-hearted* son. Even when you forget that and pull a stunt like trying to make her jealous with another girl." She smiled. "You know you're going to have to do some major groveling, don't you?"

I blew out a breath. "Yeah, I know."

"You and me both, kiddo."

I squinted at her. "Huh? Why do you need to grovel?"

Mom sighed. "Roger proposed, and I freaked. I do love him, but in that moment, I saw every one of my mistakes asking me to make them again. Not a good man who I think I could really spend my life with."

What? "I don't get it. I thought you said he broke up with you."

"See, there's that noble and loyal side of you again. I said we broke up, not that he broke up with me. I really don't deserve the pedestal you've put me on, kiddo." My mom's mouth formed a frown.

"Why?"

"Why did you end it with Aspen? Because I was scared. I thought I was ready, but I *do* know Roger is different, but I was so scared of making the same mistakes I made in the past, that I threw out my future." She patted my hand. "But this isn't about me. It's about you. Don't give up on Aspen because you're scared. We never know what's going to happen in life. Can't live in fear, or you'll never get anything."

I wanted to believe her. I wanted Aspen. "After everything, you still think it's worth it? I know you said you did, but I mean, after you bailed on Roger, do you still think love is worth all this?"

She answered quickly, surely. "Absolutely. What about you?"

Aspen popped into my head. The years of friendship. Everything she'd done for me, the laughs she'd given me and the way her face lit up when she smiled. How much she cared for her friends: Pris, Jaden and even me. And her kisses, the way I felt like all that light and energy seeped from her to me when our lips touched. The hollowness in my chest when she cried. How I didn't feel like me without her. "Hell yeah. Aspen's worth it." And she was. I would do anything to get her back.

Mom shook her head, a smirk hiding behind her frown.

"I mean, heck yeah."

"Then stop treating her like a game. This whole making her jealous thing, breaking up with her before things go too far. Be real with her. Treat her with the respect she deserves."

I nodded. "Okay, I can do that."

Mom laughed. "You're going to have to do more than that, Bastian. I'm thinking the big, grand gesture and everything."

My laugh matched hers as I rolled my eyes, but I knew I would do it. I'd do whatever it took. "What about you? Just because we're guys doesn't mean we don't like the big gesture or whatever. Are you going to get Roger back?" I asked.

"I'm not sure he'll have me." She sighed.

This time it was me who squeezed her hand. "Ma, you're talking to The Hook-up Doctor. Let me give you some advice."

* * *

I had one week to fix this before Mom was making me shut down my Hook-up Doctor blog and I'd be grounded until God knew when. I figured I deserved worse and was pretty lucky she'd given me a week at all, so I wanted to make it count. It took me a couple days to get a plan into action. This was a different kind of plan. Not the whole playing games thing, but something real. Something that my friends deserved because I figured Aspen wasn't the only person I had some pleading to do with.

One for all and all for one or something lame like that.

Jaden was first on my list.

I rarely went to Jaden's house. He never wanted to be there, so it wasn't often I went with him, and I definitely didn't go there by myself. Without him, I didn't have a car; and it was a long ass ride to make on my board. But I did it today, because I wanted my boy to know I was serious. I planned on making this up to him no matter what it took.

I jumped off my board when I came up to the gravel driveway that was almost as long as the drive from town. Why anyone would want to live in the boonies like this was beyond me. I kicked a few rocks as I made my way toward his house. I'd never tell anyone, but I always thought his driveway was a little creepy. It was practically buried in trees, all ominous and stuff. It was one of those roads, and houses for that matter, that kids got lost on in scary movies and a psycho killer was always waiting inside.

When I cleared the whack-job lane, I saw Jaden in front of his house, hiding under the hood of the beatermobile. I huffed. "All or nothing," I whispered to myself as I approached him. "Need some help?"

He didn't even turn around to look at me. "I thought you were too pretty to work on cars."

Even though he couldn't see me, I shrugged and walked to the other side of the hood and leaned in. "I am, but like you said, your beater is my beater, so I can put in a few hours of work on it." Nothing. "Plus, I figure I owe ya. You're my boy. Always been there for me. The beater, too. I guess it's time I return the favor."

Metal on metal clanked from under the hood. Jay cursed then glanced up at me. He looked like shit. His face a little pale with purple under his eyes like he hadn't slept in a while. I opened my mouth to ask if he was okay, but he cut me off. "Grab the wrench and come over here for a second. Think you can handle that, pretty boy?"

I let out a sigh of relief. Sure, to anyone else our

exchange probably didn't mean anything, but to us, we'd just said it all. He knew I was sorry, and he was letting me know he forgave me.

As I brought the wrench over to him, I couldn't stop myself from taking it further. "I didn't mean to hurt her, Jay. I do love her, and I'm going to make up for it. The thing with Crystal? It wasn't real. I didn't touch her."

Jaden stood up and looked at me, his eyes filled with something I didn't quite understand. Sadness, maybe? "Just be good to her, bro. You, Pris and Aspen?" He rubbed his face with the back of his hand. "I need you guys. I don't know what I'd do if anything screwed us up."

I nodded once, a little lost for words. We all knew things weren't good for Jaden, but in this moment, I wondered if maybe they were a lot worse than we knew. "Want to stay at my house tonight?"

He knew what I was asking, and when he replied, I knew his sarcasm was just to lighten the mood. Like I said, we were guys. It was easier that way. "You just want my help figuring out how to fix things with Pris and Aspen." He chuckled.

I laughed too. "You have no idea, bro. No idea." With that, we got to work fixing up the beatermobile.

* * *

"Dude, you're going to get my ass in as much trouble as yours." Jaden parked behind the diner I was supposed to meet Pris at. Scratch that. The diner *he* was supposed to meet Pris at, only I was going in his place. It took a little bit of begging, but I managed to get him to call Pris and ask her to meet him for dinner so that I could get to her. Pris would be a lot tougher than Jaden to make up with. The girl held a grudge like no other. Not that I didn't deserve it, but I knew I couldn't just walk up to her house and get her to forgive me without groveling. And I definitely wasn't doing this somewhere private. It would be much harder for her to kill me and bury the body if we were in a public place.

"I know. I owe you one, Jay."

"Pfft. You owe me more than one." He put the car in park. "Want me to wait?"

Pushing the door opened, I stopped and faced him. "Nah. If she catches you out here, I don't want you to fall to the same fate I probably will. Go ahead and go to my house. I called Mom, and she knows you're going over. If I'm not home in a couple hours, send a search party."

"She's not that bad. She just likes to take care of her friends. Nothing wrong with that."

I bumped Jaden's fist with my own. "Cat'cha later."

"Later," he mumbled as I got out of the car.

Jogging around the front of the building, I stopped by the coffee shop and ordered a caramel latte. I hated those froo-froo drinks, but I knew it was Pris's favorite. Or maybe I was hoping I'd get kicked out of the restaurant for sneaking a drink inside before I had to face her. Either way, ten minutes later I was holding the coffee behind my back and sneaking through the diner (someone was looking out for me because she had her back to the door) until I got to her table.

Before I lost my huevos I slipped in the booth across from her. I stilled when my eyes met hers. She looked good. Damn good, with her hair all done and make-up on her face. I couldn't pretend to know exactly what she'd done differently, because obviously make-up wasn't my thing, but it was pretty clear she'd put in some extra effort. The light in her brown eyes dimmed when she saw it was me, and I had a feeling it had to do with a lot more than just her anger at me over Aspen. I groaned. How did I not see this before? "Don't be mad at Jaden. I made him do it."

"Whatever, Bastian. Like I care. Both of you can get lost as far as I'm concerned." Her voice broke, and she went to stand up, but I grabbed her hand.

"Wait. Please, just give me a chance to explain."

She closed her eyes and let out a breath before looking at me again. "Please, Pris." I held up the drink. "I brought you a caramel latte."

With a sigh, she sat down. "You're lucky we're in public."

"Luck had nothing to do with it. I know you, Pris. Ouch." I rubbed my shin. "Damn, I didn't think about kicking under the table."

She looked at her watch. "You have ten minutes, starting now."

Man, this was going to be harder than I thought. Right at that time the waitress came by, asking for our orders during my ten minutes. Nice. "We need a little more time. At least ten minutes to be exact." The red-haired waitress gave me a weird look before shrugging and walking away.

"Nine minutes." She stared me down, and I knew she was serious.

I didn't even give myself time to sort through what I wanted to say. "I love her. I know I screwed up, and I hurt her. I'm an asshole, and I know it, but I swear the last thing I ever wanted to do was lose Aspen." I sighed. "When I broke up with her, I was feeling sorry for myself. You know, the whole parent issue thing. I didn't think it would work because my mom and her boyfriend broke up, again. If she couldn't get love right after how many tries, how could I?" Wow . . . Maybe it was better that I hadn't rehearsed that because it was much easier to be real with her when I just let myself go. I'm sure Pris was smart enough to put two and two together when it came to my mom and know she was unlucky in love, but I'd never told her how I felt about it. It wasn't something I ever really expressed to anyone, except Aspen.

"After my dad and all the other guys. And then Roger, he said he loved her and wanted to marry her, and then Mom called before we left the beach house and told me they split, and I lost it." On a roll, I kept going. "I was pissed at him for hurting her and scared things would end up the same way with me and Aspen, so I just bailed before we got a chance to dig ourselves in too deep."

I ran a hand through my hair, and leaned on my elbow. "And then I found out she really wanted Mattie all along, and she'd never really wanted me, and it pretty much crushed me, Pris. You should have seen me. I even did the whole ice cream and romance movie thing, though if you tell anyone, I will completely deny it."

She chuckled, and some of the weight on my chest loosened.

"Crystal was an accident. I freaked when I saw them at the mall and grabbed her hand. Then, I made her pretend to date me to get Aspen jealous. I'm telling you, Pris, even if she doesn't take me back, we have to get her away from Mattie. I know he's up to no good. Crystal told me he was trying to get in her cousin's pants right before hooking up with Aspen. I'll kick his ass before I let him hurt her. What does she see in that idiot anyway?"

I was starting to get all frustrated, running both my hands through my hair. Did Aspen and Mattie make up after their fight in the park? Would she choose him over me? "It may not look like it, but I do love her. I just want to take care of her."

Pris shook her head and mumbled, "Boys are so dumb." *Mayday*! *Mayday*! I was losing her.

"What can I do, Pris? I love her and you're one of my best friends. Tell me how I can fix this?"

She frowned. "To make it better with me, all you have to do is make it better for her."

On reflex, I reached across the table and grabbed Pris's hand. She was a good friend, and I knew my dumb butt didn't deserve her. "I'll do my best. I'm going to prove to Aspen, and you, that I deserve her." Mattie's ugly mug popped into my mind. "I just hope I'm not too late."

"*Idiota.* Sometimes, I wonder about guys. No offense, Bastian, but you can all be pretty dense."

She was probably talking about me in there, too, but I couldn't shake the feeling that Jaden held a big part in this as well. *PA Rocks. PA. Pris, Aspen.* Damn, I really was dense. I had no doubt Aspen and Pris tried a two for one deal. And I'd failed her. Squeezing her hand, I said, "You know any guy would be lucky to call you his girl, don't you?"

After returning my squeeze she pulled away. "Yeah, I know. But don't get any ideas. You're in love with Aspen, remember?"

I gave her one of my best smirks. "Yeah, I know."

"Alright, I'm out of here. Go find your girl and sweep her off her feet before Matt does it for you. I have it on good authority they're supposed to be going out tomorrow night. That doesn't give you much time."

I got up and pulled Pris into a hug. "I'll walk you out," I told her. She picked up her coffee and led the way to her car. When we stopped, she was touching her necklace I'd seen her playing with on the trip. "That's nice. Parents get it for you for your birthday?"

Pris sighed. "Someone did, but not them." *Oh.* It was obvious she didn't want to tell me who it was, so I left it alone. "Need a ride?" she asked.

I shook my head. "Nah. I have some stuff to figure out."

She gave me a smile and pulled out. Before driving away she put her window down. "Oh, and Bastian?"

"Yeah?"

"If you mess this up, I'll mess you up, too."

CHAPTER SEVENTEEN

O n the way home, I spotted a familiar car by the arcade and realized I had one more person to make amends with before I could move on to making things up to Aspen. These were all a warm up. They were preparing me for the big one. Not saying I didn't take Jaden, Pris and now Crystal's apologies seriously, but somewhere along the way I realized I needed to really earn Aspen back, and these were all steps on that road. With each apology, I earned her a little more. By the time I made it to Aspen, I'd be the guy she deserved.

Or maybe I was just telling myself that to give myself a little more hope at actually getting the girl in the end. Honestly, I wasn't sure.

Crystal had actually been pretty understanding of the whole thing. I didn't go into as many details as I did with Pris, but in the end, she forgave me for misleading her about the whole break-up and even wished me luck on getting Aspen back. Kind of made me wish I knew that Will guy, because I sure wanted to knock some sense into him. She was a cool girl, and I hoped she found a guy who realized it.

The walk home pretty much sucked, but I had time to work through my whole grand gesture in my head. On reflex, I looked two doors down as I stepped onto my porch. Damn, I was such a sap. Even her house looked different to me, now. I wondered if that would ever change. If everything about her would always be . . . brighter, now. Okay, so maybe brighter wasn't the right word. It sounded a little lame, but . . . more? Yeah, everything about her was just *more* now.

Shaking my head because I'd officially lost my mind, I turned to open my front door. Something caught my eye, and I turned back to her house.

And then dropped to the porch so no one could see me. Yep, definitely lost my mind because here I was, lying on my stomach and peeking through railing on my porch so I could see her—with *him.*

Get up, Bastian. You're officially a peeping Tom now. Only I couldn't. They looked like they were both in a much better mood than they'd been when I last saw them together. My skin started to crawl and feel all prickly.

It all happened so quickly. She was smiling. He shrugged, but not in the asshole kind of way. Then he held his arms open, and she stepped inside.

Mattie was hugging her. Hugging my girl. The one I'd pretty much thrown away and there was nothing I could do about it. Honestly, I probably deserved it. It wasn't a long hug, and afterward, he turned and walked away, shooting one last glance over his shoulder and smiling at her. Aspen watched him drive away, then turned and went back into her house.

My stomach knotted. For the first time, I really let myself consider the fact that I might not get her back. That she just might feel the same way about Mattie that I felt about her.

I might have really lost her. But no matter what, I wasn't going to give up. Even if I walked away from this in pieces, she was worth it.

THE HOOK-UP DOCTOR
HELPING GIRLS GET THEIR DREAM GUYS SINCE . . . WELL, HOW LONG ISN'T IMPORTANT. WHAT MATTERS IS I'M GOOD. AND I AM.

Okay, so I know this blog is usually used just for contact information and stuff, but this is important. You see, in a few days The Hook-up Doctor is officially retiring. I could go into a million different reasons as to why, one being that my mom found out and said

I have to, but the fact is, if I wanted to keep it going, I could. There are always ways, if you know what I mean. The truth is, I'm quitting because I'm a scam.

Yeah, I have a good track record. I've pretty much hooked-up everyone who contacted me, but the point is, I never believed in this. I mean, I never promised more than just a hook-up, but I did let people believe that I was really giving them more. That I really felt like they could get love out of all this, when to me, love had always been a bigger scam than I was.

And then, you guessed it . . . I fell in love.

Let me tell you, love isn't a scam. It's real, overpowering and fierce. It has the power to make you feel like nothing can stop you. Like you can do anything, and it also has the ability to break you. And the even crazier part is, you can break it, too. Or ruin it, I guess, because it sure as hell doesn't just go away. Believe me. I know.

You see, the girl I fell in love with? She seriously rocks. That's not even a strong enough word, but I don't want to get too mushy in this. I'll save that stuff for when I beg her for forgiveness. But yeah, she was amazing; and being with her, it felt right in a way I hadn't known I was missing before her.

And I wrecked it. I didn't trust what I was feeling. I got scared. Yep, I'm not afraid to admit that shit. I was scared—half that I would hurt her and the other half scared she would hurt me, so I did exactly what I didn't want to do, and I told her goodbye.

It hurt. I felt like half a man, and for a guy like me, someone who has more pride than I probably should, that didn't fly.

I won't bore you with all the details (who am I kidding with the bore thing. I'm sure you guys want all the details). I'm not going to share them. They're between us, but I will say, I didn't keep it at one screw up. I had a few big ones. I'm not proud of any of it, but through it all, I still love her.

The even cooler part is, somehow, through it all, I love her more. I also realize that loving her is worth whatever happens (yeah, my girl is that cool). Even if she can't forgive me for playing games, and not treating her the way I should have, I'm not sorry I fell for her. What I'm feeling is more real than anything else out there. It's better than hook-ups, and scoping girls out at the mall, and flirting and all that other stuff I used to live for.

And even though I know there are no guarantees in life, I'll risk the possible pain and the possibility that some day it could end, if she'll give me a chance now. What's the point in protecting yourself when it keeps you from feeling anything? That's what I realized. Without her, I wasn't really feeling.

So, as I say goodbye to all the readers out there, I hope you'll consider what I've said. Believe me; I know what I'm talking about. I said that before, but this time it's for real. And if she's reading this, I'm going to make it up to you. Even if it's too late, I have to tell you how I feel. You know me. I have a knack for getting what I want, so you should just give in now. ;)

Not really. But honestly, I'm sorry I screwed up, and I'm going to tell you in person. I just hope I don't break my neck in the progress. Oh, and if I do, I'm going to tell you now, I love you.

S.

* * *

The night after writing my blog, I stood on the side of Aspen's house, looking up at the mountain of a climb I had in front of me. Okay, so it wasn't a mountain, but standing under her window, it definitely felt like one. I shook my hands and exhaled, grabbed the lattice, and pulled myself up. I took it slowly, hoping the thing was really as solid as it looked. Following what I'd always heard, I didn't look down as I climbed higher and higher.

The thing is, the real reason I never would climb through her damn window, no matter how many times she asked me, was because I wasn't real fond of heights. The one time with Alex's window, it had been the climb or her dad and a baseball bat. Plus, I didn't really have much time to think about it. Now, I had plenty of time, but I kept going. And I really, *really* hoped she was in her room. Alone. Oh, and while I was hoping, I also prayed she saw my blog post from last night.

Before I knew it, I was two stories up and outside her bedroom window. My first instinct was to open the dumb thing and jump inside. The faster I could get in, the safer I would be, but decided I better knock because, knowing my luck, she'd be in there getting dressed or with Mattie or something. The last thing I needed was to get in a fight with her boyfriend after sneaking in her bedroom or look like I was trying to get an eyeful.

Before I could chicken out, I held on tight with my right hand and knocked on her window with my left. I counted to five, and knocked again. Yeah, I knew I wasn't being very patient, but I was the one hanging two stories in the air here.

The curtains slid open and green eyes met mine. My heart immediately starting pounding away. And then she slid the window open and walked away. "Here goes nothing," I whispered to myself before pulling my way inside. "Hey." *Totally lame, Bastian.*

"Hey." She sat on the edge of her bed, wearing a pair of shorts and a tank top.

I gave the room the once over to make sure her door was shut. It was. "So yeah. I finally climbed through your window."

She nodded, picking at her finger nail. "I saw your blog."

My heart raced, and I was scared to death, but I came here to do something, and no matter what happened, I'd see through to my side of it. "My mom told me to go with the big, grand gesture. I wracked my mind trying to think of something perfect to do, but I just couldn't come up with anything. All that stuff . . . it's not really you. You're real, and I wanted to do something that was real. Not really for show, you know? Something simple that I knew would mean something to you. So, yeah, hence the window. I hope it's okay."

For the first time since I came into her room, she looked at me. I mean, really looked at me and those zaps and sparks went off beneath my skin. But still, she didn't speak.

"I never meant for things to turn out the way they did, Woodstock. That weekend at the beach? It was perfect, and then Mom called and told me she and Roger broke up and it scared the shit out of me. I'm not going to pretend that's an excuse, because it's not. I should have trusted you. Trusted us and not assumed we'd end up like them, but I did, and I'm sorry. The last thing I ever wanted to do was walk away from you, but I'm human and I screwed up. Big time. I tried to tell myself I was protecting you, but I was really protecting me."

I stepped closer to her, but stopped. I didn't want to push things. "Not very noble of me, I know. You had the ability to pulverize me, so I bailed, and it was wrong. And Crystal?" I ran a hand through my hair and sighed in frustration. "That was a big screw up, but I swear to you, there was nothing going on with us. She's in love with some other guy, and we were talking and ended up at the mall together. Then, I saw you with Mattie, and I knew what my mom felt like all those times she'd had her heart broken. It was dumb, but I just reacted and grabbed her hand, but I wanted it to be you. It felt wrong touching someone else like that, Woodstock."

I took a couple breaths, giving her the time to speak. Willing her to say something, but she didn't so I kept going. This time, I didn't hold myself back. I walked up to her and knelt on the ground between her legs. "I know I'm probably too late. That you're with Mattie, and if he makes you happy, I want that for you, but I had to tell you, I love you. Being the Hook-up Doctor, I thought I knew everything. I was wrong. I prided myself on knowing what I wanted, when I never really did. Now, I know what I want. It's you. Only you. Even if you don't really want me that way, and I'm too late, I need to know you forgive me, Woodstock. You're my best friend." I didn't stop there. I wasn't going to hold anything back from her.

"But I gotta say, I really freakin' hope you love me, too. Oh, and if you do, I'd love it if you gave me permission to kick Mattie's ass. I think that would help me heal." With that one, I got the response I wanted. Her lips stretched into a smirk. It wasn't a real smile, but it was a start.

I risked a slap across the face to raise my hand and cup her cheek. "More than anything else, I just want you."

"Did you kiss her?" she whispered.

"Hell no. These lips belong to you."

She smiled again. Reaching up, she pushed a strand of hair behind her ear. "I didn't either. Kiss Matt, I mean. I was hurt, and I used him to try and get over it. See, I can't really be mad at you about the whole Crystal thing, because I did the same thing with Matt. I mean, it wasn't like I really set out to make you jealous, but I used him to get over you."

Thump. Thump. Thump. I could hardly hear her over the blood pulsing in my ears. "Did you? Get over me?"

Aspen chuckled. "Sebastian, I've loved you since we were five years old and you downed the whole glass of soy milk, pretending to like it just so you didn't hurt my feelings."

I'm not afraid to admit it, I pretty much saw stars at that moment. She loved me and nothing was taking that away from me.

"After a while, I never thought you would feel the same. You were always going for girls like Alex the tramp, so I pretty much gave up. I really did contact The Hook-up Doctor to help me get with

Matt. I figured if you didn't need me, I'd find a way not to need you. But then things got weird. When you took care of me at the party, and the night in my room. My brain started to get all fuzzy, and I didn't know what I wanted anymore. I was scared to hope you were starting to feel the same, but it was also like things shifted for us, ya know?"

Ah, so that's what the second thoughts thing in her messages had been about. Silently, I thanked God. I rubbed my thumb over her cheek. I'd forgotten how soft her skin was. "Yeah, I know. That's how I felt when I realized I was falling for you, too. Like things shifted."

"I invited Matt over yesterday." My hand stilled. *Please let this go my way.* "I admitted to him that I was in love with you. It didn't feel right, and I wanted to call it off." *Exhale breath.* "He was okay with it, and admitted he was seeing someone else anyway. Guess you were right about him. Wasn't like I could be mad, since it made my skin crawl when he tried to hold my hand. We hugged and agreed to go our separate ways."

That's what the hug had been! I couldn't help it. I laughed.

"What's so funny?" Aspen asked.

"I've been driving myself crazy. I saw you guys. I

246

used my ninja skills I'm always telling you about and kind of spied on you. From my porch. While I laid on my stomach, peeking through the railing." Wow, that sounded even lamer out loud than it felt when I'd done it.

Aspen laughed, too. One of her hands came up and ran through my hair, the way only she could. "What am I going to do with you?"

"Hmmm." I smiled. "Forgive me? Love me? Kiss me?"

"Are you sure you want to? I mean, my parents are considering the move to a hippie commune. I'm not sure they'll let me date you since you don't live in an energy efficient house. Maybe after my dad hypnotizes you during meditation, he'll change his mind."

I dropped my head back and rubbed a hand over my face. "Mattie told you about that, huh?"

"Yeah . . . You're a trip, Bastian. How did you come up with that?" She smiled.

"No clue. I just knew I'd do anything to keep him away from you. It made me sick to my stomach to think of him and you together."

Aspen stroked my hair again. "Ugh, are you trying to pull some of your moves on me?" Her words were playful.

"Depends. Is it working?"

Aspen licked her lips, and I could have sworn I felt it. "I don't know. You're The Hook-up Doctor. Aren't you supposed to be, like, all-knowing?"

"I don't know anything except that I love you. Oh, and that I want to be your boyfriend, and I'm still kind of holding out that you'll let me beat up Mattie."

"I love you, too. Yes and no."

"I can handle two out of three." Then I leaned forward and pressed my lips to hers, and it felt as good as I thought it would. Our lips moved together perfectly. A perfect match. Because we had skills like that.

EPILOGUE

I slid my finger in the collar of my shirt and tugged. "I feel like a friggin' idiot." I groaned. "Seriously, this shit is choking me. Want to go upstairs with me and help me out of my shirt?" Smirking, I looked down at Aspen, tucked against my side. She rolled her eyes, obviously not thinking my little stripping idea was as good as I did.

"Bastian! It's your mom's engagement party." She licked her lips and I couldn't help but lean forward and press a kiss to them.

"Yeah, *her* engagement party. Not mine. Why do I have to get all dressed up too?" I'd vetoed the whole suit thing, but somehow got roped into slacks and a white, button-up dress shirt. If I had to wear this for the party, I knew there was no way I could get out of a tux for the wedding.

Aspen slid out from under my arm to stand in front of me. She wrapped her arms around my waist. "Hmm, well I think you look pretty hot."

"Don't I always look hot?" I linked my hands

together behind her neck. She was wearing a really sexy skirt. It hung right above her knees, not showing too much skin, but enough to drive me wild. Aspen always drove me wild. In more ways than one. In the month since we'd gotten together, I'd realized just how much work relationships could be, but I wouldn't change it for anything. She was my girl and I loved her.

"You're so conceited." She chuckled.

"Yeah, but you love me anyway. Feel free to tell me how sexy I am any time though. A guy can never hear it enough—ouch! You pinched me."

"I didn't say sexy, I said hot."

"But you think I'm sexy too. I know it." Leaning forward I pressed another kiss to her lips. "I know I think you are."

She rolled her eyes and I laughed.

A slow song started to play and I pulled away from the wall, bringing Aspen with me. "Dance with me?"

She nodded her head. Our arms switched places, hers weaving around my neck and mine wrapped around her waist as we started to sway to the music. I heard a loud, familiar laugh and looked over to see Roger dipping my mom.

"She's so happy, Bastian. I've never seen her like

this." Aspen gave me a squeeze before leaning her head against my chest.

"Yeah, she is, huh?" I smiled at Mom even though she wasn't looking my way. It felt so damn good to see her so happy. The weight I'd carried in my chest for so long was gone now. "You know, I'll never admit it, but I actually like Roger. He's a good guy and I really think he loves her. Of course, I still have my eye on him. If he breaks her heart I'll break his nose, but," I shrugged, "everything just kind of feels like it's going to be okay now, ya know?"

Aspen pulled far enough away to look me in the eyes. "You have such a big heart, Sebastian Dale Hawkins."

"Shh, don't tell anyone that either."

"Your secrets are safe with me."

I buried my face in her hair, to hide from the seriously mushy words that were about to come out of my mouth. "And your heart is safe with me."

We were quiet for a few more minutes, just holding each other and dancing. Suddenly, Aspen was talking again, her voice low and hurt. "She loves him, you know."

I was a little confused. Hadn't we already talked about Mom loving Roger? "What?"

She tilted her head to the side and I saw Pris

standing in the corner. It had been a bumpy ride between her and Jaden for the past month. She was my one failed hook-up and it still killed me. Especially after seeing her face when it had been me to show up at the diner and not Jaden. I never would have gone that route if I would have known how she felt. They were always civil to each other, but things were different now. There was always this kind of tension around us. "I know. Makes me feel like shit."

"It's not your fault," she told me. "I just wish things would go back to the way they were, or that Jaden would pull his head out."

"I think he's going through some stuff."

"Yeah, well she is too. I mean, they're best friends. Why can't they just help each other?"

The song faded, another slow song starting in its place. "Well, you know, I've been known to hook-up a person or two . . ."

"Oh, no. Don't you even think about it, Bastian. I want them together too, but playing The Hook-up Doctor just makes a mess of things. We need to let them figure it out on their own."

I shrugged. "Maybe. Maybe not."

I looked over at Jaden sitting about twenty feet away from Pris. His eyes were on her the same way I used to watch Aspen. Then he stood up and walked over to her. They talked and then he eased her just as close to himself as I held Aspen right now.

And then, without a sliver of space between them, they danced.

Read on for a taster of the companion
novel to *What a Boy Wants* . . .

WHAT A BOY NEEDS

CHAPTER ONE

I stiffen. Heat rips through my body like someone injected it into my veins. It starts in my chest, cracking and crystalizing my insides as it spreads. There's a part of me, the smart part, that knows I'm being an idiot. I'm freaking out when I don't have a right to. But there's the other part, the one that hides deep inside of me so I can pretend it doesn't exist, that knows it should be *me* sitting with Priscilla right now. My hand in her hair. My lips on her neck. I should be stealing food off her lunch plate and saying something stupid because it's so like *us* for her to be pissed at me.

I've been making her mad ever since that time in kindergarten when she yelled at me for Sebastian's lame ass pulling Aspen's ponytail. Aspen started chasing Bastian like she was supposed to, since he's the one who did it, but Pris narrowed those dark eyes at me like it was my fault, before she charged.

I let her catch me.

I like it when she catches me.

But last summer, she stopped chasing. It sucks.

So does my internal monologue every time I see her. It's really starting to piss me off. I've gone soft and I hate it, but I can't seem to make myself do anything about it, either. Instead I grin, talk shit to Bastian, tease Aspen, and pretend it doesn't tear me up every time I look at her. That I don't know it's my own damn fault, and that there's nothing I can do to change it. It's for the best.

In case you haven't caught on, it's been a long school year.

The Pris dating Craig thing is new, but it doesn't feel like it.

I want my fist to meet his nose. Multiple times.

Aren't I just peachy?

I've become a serious buzz kill. Priscilla, Sebastian, Aspen, and I have been tight forever. It's always been the four of us, but last summer Sebastian fell for Aspen. It was only a matter of time anyway and it's cool. I'm happy for them and all that, but it's made stuff for Priscilla and me tough because I want to be with her, too. I want her way more than I should, but I also realize it's a no go. She deserves way better. For her sake, I hate that it took her so long to realize it.

Someone slams into my back, making me stumble.

I whip around and take a swing at Sebastian, which he dodges, bouncing on the balls of his feet to try and look like he's some kind of heavyweight boxer.

"Don't make me take you out, *Doc*," I tease. The whole thing with him and Aspen started because Sebastian ran some stupid, anonymous business online where he called himself the Hook-up Doctor. Aspen contacted him to hook her up with this idiot who used to work at the pizza place with them, only he didn't know it was her and she didn't know it was him. He started to fall for her and everything was all set for a movie-ending happily ever after until he pulled a bonehead-Sebastian move.

It all worked out in the end because if he wasn't so blind, he would have known they wanted each other probably since that day in kindergarten. Priscilla and I were his only failed hook-up.

I slam the door on those thoughts.

"Please, I could take you with my eyes closed—shit, ouch," Sebastian limps after accidentally stepping on Aspen's foot.

"Hello? *You* stepped on *me*. I should be the one saying ouch!" She pushes a strand of her light brown hair behind her ear. Sebastian buries his face in her neck the same way Craig just did with Pris. Aspen's hand threads through his black hair.

"Sorry, baby," Bastian leans forward. "Gimme a kiss. My lips have healing power."

Aspen swoons and I almost vomit in my mouth. "Healing power? Did I mention I fell on my ass this morning? It hurts right here." I turn and point to my left cheek. Sebastian tries to kick me, but I jerk out of his way, laughing.

"Ha, ha." He smirks. He knows that was a good joke. He just doesn't want to admit it.

"You're just jealous I thought of it."

We fall in line together as the three of us head toward Priscilla at our table. Pris sitting with her boyfriend at the table that's belonged to the four of us since our freshman year.

Seriously, it's like I can't stop those little comments from body-slamming their way into my brain. This isn't supposed to be the way it works. I'm not sure *how* it was supposed to work since I've always known I couldn't go there. Not with her, even though she makes my pulse jack-hammer. But before, I could ignore it. After all the shit went down with Aspen and Sebastian last summer—after I found out she tried to find a way to make me see her in a different light—it makes things a whole hell of a lot harder to ignore.

I've always seen her. Always.

I've just been trying not to.

"What's up?" I fall onto the bench across from them. I give her a little nod, but don't pay attention to the douche. Really? Craig? He's always been a clown. I don't know what she sees in him.

After twisting the top off my Cherry Pepsi, I down a drink.

"Hey, Jay," Pris replies, but gives her attention to Aspen. "Did you finish your math homework?"

"Pris, you realize we graduate in two weeks, right?" Sebastian cuts in. "I'm pretty sure there's a coolness rule that says you're not supposed to do homework anymore. It's expected and shit."

Aspen nudges him. "*I* did my homework."

"Guess Jay and I are the only cool ones, then."

We hit fists. "Not really a newsflash, B." We both laugh while the girls roll their eyes like they always do. Craig's on his phone playing whatever his game of the week is. He's always on his phone when he's around us. It might or might not be because Sebastian and I don't really pay any attention to him. Probably not a very cool thing to do, but I seriously can't stand to look at the guy and Bastian's just tight like that. He's my boy and it's in our code to always have each other's backs. I'm sure he's cool to Craig when I'm not around, but just like I never would have been tight with Mattie, the guy Aspen got with for a little bit last year, Bastian wouldn't hang me out to dry either.

Plus, I'm pretty sure Craig dislikes us as much as we dislike him.

Something catches my eye and I look over to see Craig pull out a pack of gum and push a piece of spearmint into his mouth.

"Want one, Priscilla?" He holds the pack out to her.

Hearing him call her Priscilla makes me want to go nuts.

Douche.

The way Sebastian smirks and turns his head to look at me, I realize I must have said that out loud. Oops. Not.

"Jaden!" Priscilla's voice is tight. It's different when she's mad at me now. Before it was just *us* and it was never real anger and now it's . . . hell, I don't know. It's just different.

She turns to Craig and takes the piece of gum he offered her. I can't believe she actually puts it in her mouth, just to spite me.

Yep. That's my clue to get out of here.

I push to my feet. "See ya after school, Bastian." I turn to Craig. "Ever since she got sick off Peppermint

Schnapps last year, Spearmint makes her feel like she's going to puke."

I shove my hands into my pockets. Without another word, I'm out.

Don't miss Jaden's story…

WHAT A BOY NEEDS

Jaden Sinclair knows he'll never amount to anything… so why
would he deserve a girl like Priscilla Mendoza?

Since last summer things have been screwed up between Jaden
and Pris. He knows it's his fault, but that doesn't stop him from
wanting to go a few rounds with her new boyfriend. He also
knows he's the loser his dad calls him, but it doesn't stop him
from wanting her.

After getting a huge bomb dropped on him, Jaden lashes out and
lands himself in jail. Everything in his chaotic life is turned upside
down and to make it worse, his mom kicks him out in order to side
with his dad. Yeah, he's totally a prize for a girl like Pris.

Sebastian, Aspen and Pris are all going places in their lives, and
Jaden knows he can't keep tagging along for the ride.

The group has one last chance for The Epic Adventure they've
been looking for: a road trip to New York, where Jaden's
friends will be going to college. Unfortunately, the more time
Jaden hangs around Pris, the harder it is to keep the carefully
constructed walls between them so she doesn't find out what a
train wreck he really is.

When the trip ends, Jaden has to decide if he's ready to say
goodbye to his friends, and the girl he loves. He knows what he
needs, but will he be man enough to go for it?

headline
ETERNAL